MAN ON THE MOUNTAIN

Gladys Hasty Carroll

Filled with the warmth and the deft characterizations that are Gladys Hasty Carroll's special genius, this allegorical tale tells of a future in which citizens are segregated according to age. There are four divisions. The groups do not communicate, but live in fear and suspicion – until two children somehow get into Old State, where the elderly live. Two of the residents undertake a journey to find the parents, and the message they carry to the other States forms the theme of the book.

Novels in Large Print
by Gladys Hasty Carroll

AS THE EARTH TURNS

MAN ON THE MOUNTAIN

NEXT OF KIN

Man On The Mountain

GLADYS HASTY CARROLL

John Curley & Associates, Inc.
South Yarmouth, Ma.

Library of Congress Cataloguing in Publication Data

Carroll, Gladys Hasty, 1904–
Man on the mountain.

Originally published: Boston: Little, Brown, 1969.
1. Large type books. I. Title.
[PS3505.A77533M3 1982] 813′.52 81–12542
ISBN 0–89340–369–5 AACR2

Published in Large Print by arrangement with Gladys Hasty Carroll.

Distributed in the U.K. and Commonwealth by Magna Print Books.

Printed in Great Britain

To
the memory of
my
grandparents

Time: **The mid-21st century.**

Scene: **A continent roughly the size and shape of Australia, named Great Country in honor of Great Mountain which rises to a mighty peak near its center. Great Country is composed of four States, each separated from neighbor States by invisible barriers which can be penetrated only by supersonic jets.**

PART ONE: Man on the Mountain

Setting: **A child's world, the one world inhabited by humans which has never changed and will never change and forever holds the hope of the race. "Except ye become as a little child . . ."**

PART TWO: The Grammies and the Grampies

Setting: **Old State: no resident is less**

than sixty years of age.

PART THREE: The Mommies and the Daddies

Setting: **Two State, where children under twelve live with parents between the ages of thirty and forty or so.**

PART FOUR: The Guys and the Dolls

Setting: **Midway: the location of boarding schools for those of preparatory school age; the seat of Great Country government, heart of its industrial complex, communication and transportation systems, and military establishment; home of citizens between forty and sixty.**

PART FIVE: The Kids

Setting: **New State, occupied by those between sixteen and thirty.**

PART SIX: The State and the Nation

I Man on the Mountain

My story begins with the day little Dunwoodie Keogh ran away.

It is said that once upon a time Great Country, which surrounds Great Mountain and reaches out from its base in all directions to the sea, was four separate countries, each named for the skin color of its inhabitants. But long ago the massive walls dividing Brown Land, White Land, Black Land, and Yellow Land were taken down and all sentry boxes destroyed. The people took the name of their mountain as the name of their country, now a loose federation of four states. The first names given to the states were North, South, East, and West, but quite a while ago they came to be known as Old State, New State, Midway, and Two State.

Little Dunwoodie lived in Two State, and one day he ran away.

Strangely enough, the razed walls have been mysteriously replaced by partitions of a material similar to plastic. No one knows who set them up, nor exactly when. They are invisible but impenetrable. Some openings were left in these partitions, and these have never been policed, but have been so rarely found and used in recent years that they are overgrown by alder bushes. The citizens of Great Country are now divided according to the age of their bodies. When they must communicate across the boundaries – which is increasingly seldom – they do so by airwaves.

The old, of course, live in Old State, facing north; the newly independent in New State – once South – where all the colleges are, and the small furnished apartments, the paperback bookshops, the coffeehouses, and the sidewalk art exhibits. Midway is the eastern state of restless, enigmatic preparatory school students and their busy, baffled parents. Two State, west of Great

Mountain, is occupied by families with preschool or grade school children, and so is the only part of Great Country in which two generations live together in harmony, characteristically fearing nothing so much as being separated from each other.

Dunwoodie was in his fifth year the day he ran away.

There was a great to-do when he could not be found. All the young mothers, in Bermuda shorts, faded madras shirts, and thonged sandals, hurried here and there pushing strollers across bridges in the parks and into the tall grass of vacant lots calling and looking for Dunwoodie while calling to their own runabouts to be sure of not losing them. When Dunwoodie was not found in any of the places he had ever been, the young mothers called the young fathers at their work and the young fathers told their friends, and soon the offices and stores were all but deserted and cars were being driven hither and yon in search of Dunwoodie, with the police alerted throughout the state. But there was no trace of Dunwoodie anywhere.

Of course everyone asked his mother many questions.

They asked her when she had last seen Dunwoodie, and she said it was about nine o'clock in the morning when she was arranging flowers in her Paul Revere bowl. He had been playing on the other side of the picture window since breakfast and had come in to tell her the cat had just caught a mouse. She had said, "Really? What a clever old puss!" and gone on pushing an obstinate Japanese pink between two stalks of blue delphinium. When, this accomplished, she had looked up, he was gone, and she had not seen him since.

They asked her what he was wearing, and what he had eaten for breakfast, and how much he weighed, and if he was friendly with strangers, and if he had ever disappeared before; and they asked to see pictures of him. She had books and books full of pictures of him, and reels and reels of movies of him, and everybody looked at them and his mother cried and so did some of the other mothers. She said he had never disappeared before, and he was very shy, and that morning he had been wearing little green corduroy pants, a white shirt, and a green cap with a long red feather his father and mother had bought for him at the beach. Then everybody went out again looking everywhere for Dunwoodie Keogh, or at very least for a green cap with a long red feather.

But by dusk they had not found even a long red feather, and it was at that time that the people who were looking for him first heard that one of the Ryan children at the other side of town had also disappeared.

Now the Ryans were in many ways different from the Keoghs. Their house was just as well built, as all houses are well built in Great Country, and it and the grounds around it were larger because there were so many more Ryans. There were the twins Tommy and Teddy Ryan, and the twins Patty and Pammy Ryan, and Chuck Ryan and Pete Ryan and Kathy Ryan and nobody was quite sure how many Ryan babies unless their mother was, and she may not have been for she was a great reader. When she and Bob Ryan moved to Two State to await the arrival of Tommy and Teddy, they had had cartons and cartons and cartons of paperbacks flown in from New State with them, and every month or so she ordered another carton. Sue Ryan was a happy woman, sitting contentedly in her big chair growing babies and reading her little books. She saw no need of knowing just where her children were, since they always knew where she was. They went where they pleased all the daylight hours, carrying crackers, picking wild fruit, drinking from jugs of Popsi they kept hidden among bushes, napping in treehouses they built from the boards Bob kept bringing home from the lumberyard for which he was a truck driver.

But that night when Bob Ryan came home at dusk – as he always did because by then Sue had put aside her book – and counted the children in their beds (it was his habit, for some reason, to count the older ones; he never noticed the babies) he frowned, counted them again, and went downstairs to tell Sue somebody was missing; he thought it was Chuck.

They woke up Tommy and Teddy, sent them out to look for their brother, and sat down at the kitchen table to drink coffee and eat the Napoleons Bob had brought home. Sue looked beautiful in her rosy housecoat, even eating a Napoleon, even by fluorescent light; as beautiful as any woman in another time candlelit in a dinner gown. Another baby would be coming any day now.

Tommy and Teddy found many people on the street looking for Dunwoodie and told them all that they were looking for Chuck. Soon those who weren't asking the Keoghs questions were coming to ask the Ryans questions.

By now the Keoghs were very much distressed. Doctors were pressing sedatives upon Mrs. Keogh. The Ryans were not in the least distressed. They said Chuck knew how to take care of himself, and wherever he was he was all right. Sue supposed he had been wearing dungarees and a T-shirt. The parents of both boys agreed that Dunwoodie and Chuck almost certainly did not know each other and, since they lived on opposite sides of the city, there was not one chance in a million that they were together.

But they were.

Dunwoodie had run right around the corner of the house where he lived and right off the block where he lived and right away as fast as he could from everyone he knew, toward Great Mountain where he had never been and where he supposed nobody was.

But Chuck was there, climbing a birch tree to swing back to the ground, and he looked down and saw that Dunwoodie was crying.

"What's up, kid?" he asked. "Bee sting you?"

Dunwoodie shook his head, and ran on. Chuck swung down and ran after him. He could have caught up with him sooner, for he was a year older and more than a year faster, but he kept slowing down to kick sideways at roots or stopping to see if he could pry up a rock. He was atisfied just to stay in sight of the red feather on Dunwoodie's cap, until a branch knocked off the cap and Dunwoodie left it lying there on the moss and ran on. Then Chuck picked up the cap, put it on his own shaggy round head, and overtook Dunwoodie.

"Lookit! Got your cap!" he shouted, circling around Dunwoodie. "Betcha can't take it back! Betcha!"

"Don't want it," sobbed Dunwoodie, slowing to a walk.

Chuck was flabbergasted. A kid that had a green cap with a long red feather not want it?

He took it off and held it out to Dunwoodie.

"You can have it," he said. "It's yours."

Dunwoodie raised a small dark fist and struck the cap out of Chuck's hand.

"Told you I didn't want it," he said.

They were standing still now, the cap lying on a juniper bush beside Chuck.

"Cripes, kid," said Chuck. "Looks brand-new to me. What's the matter with it?"

"It's from Them," said Dunwoodie.

He kicked the cap off the juniper bush. It went a little way into the air, came down on the edge of the visor, and would have rolled over the ledge if Chuck had not been such a fast runner. Chuck sat down in a mossy place, put the cap on his knee, and made a ring of his grubby thumb and forefinger to pull the red feather through. It was wet from the bushes and felt soft and tickly, like a dog's tongue.

"Who's Them?" he asked curiously.

Dunwoodie slumped down, hid his

face in his hunched knees, finished his crying, ground out the last of the tears with the heels of his hands, and began to talk.

He said Them were the people he had lived with as long as he could remember, people who kept a big animal with long claws and sharp teeth that grabbed any nice little mouse that came along and bit it and let it go and bit it again until it was dead and then ate it. He had not known until today that the Cat would do a thing like that, but They had known it. They liked to have it do it. When he told Them what had happened, They just said, "What a clever old puss." Were the people Chuck lived with like that? Was that why he had run away, too?

Chuck said, "I didn't run away. I don't think." And then he asked, "What's 'clever'?"

"Smart," said Dunwoodie. "Like me. Because I can read. They say, 'Listen to Dunwoodie. You know, he's really clever.'"

"Can you read?" asked Chuck,

amazed.

"Sure. Can't you?"

"Course not. My mother does. All the time."

"Does she have a Cat?"

"No, but a lot of them come around."

"Would she let them do that to mice?"

"She lets anybody do anything they want to. She's reading. Even if you ask her anything, she don't hear you. You have to poke her. Even then she most usually don't really hear."

Chuck was not complaining. He was just explaining. He knew cats caught mice, and birds, too. He supposed they had to. He supposed they were hungry. It was awful to be hungry. He knew, too, that when mice and rats got into the cellar in the winter they gnawed into the vegetables and raced through the partitions and sometimes made plaster fall. He could not remember that he had ever met a nice little mouse.

"That's another thing," said Dunwoodie. "They don't hear you.

They don't listen. When you try to talk to them they go right on thinking what they were thinking before. I'm not going back."

"Neither am I," said Chuck.

He meant, not now. Not until he got hungry. Or sleepy. He knew it was still morning, for he could feel his breakfast in him; and he had crackers buttoned into his pocket. He was a little thirsty, but he knew there was a spring not far away. He had been here before.

"Let's climb higher," said Chuck. "Betcha I can find us a spring to drink from."

"What's a spring?"

"Water bubbling up in a hole in the ground. You lay flat like you are now and put your mouth in. It's icy, icy. It goes up your nose and runs down your chin. It's fun. Come on."

Chuck clapped the feathered cap over his shock of sandy hair and raced off, but was careful not to go so fast that Dunwoodie would lose sight of him. He staged a grand hunt for that spring, knowing where it was all the time. He made a fine pretense of throwing back his head like a hound and sniffing for the smell of water, running toward the spring but just skirting it, claiming the scent was growing fainter, and running back again at a slant.

"It's strong now, Dun," shouted Chuck. "We *must* be close now. . . ." Almost going to fall into it, we must be. . . . Oops! Here it is! Sure as you're born, Dun, here's the bubbliest little spring you ever saw! Right here!" He pulled off the cap and waved it in circles.

Dunwoodie stumbled up, panting and hot. They threw themselves on their stomachs and drank deep, their two heads touching, one dark and curly, the other a sandy mop.

When they were saturated, Dunwoodie sat back on his haunches and stared at Chuck.

"I sure wish I could learn to find water," he said. "I never smelled a thing different, no matter what way we went. Honest. Could you teach me?"

"Guess not. Guess you can or you can't. Like reading. But you don't need to know how, Dun, long as you stick with Old Chuck. I'll do it for both of us."

"Same's I'll read for both of us. If we find anything that has to be read."

"It's a deal, Dun."

"We're partners, Chuck!"

A partner was something Dunwoodie realized now he had needed for quite a while. Chuck did not know what a partner was, but he hoped it was a kind of twin. He had always wanted a twin.

He threw an arm across Dunwoodie's shoulders.

"We ought to make a mark in blood," he said. "Tommy and Teddy did. But we haven't got any paper. And we haven't got a pin."

"Let's go 'way up there and build a house, Chuck."

Dunwoodie pointed toward the highest peak. Chuck looked, and hesitated.

"Why don't we build it here by the spring?"

"We haven't gone far enough. They might catch us here. You can find us another spring at the top."

Chuck was not altogether sure of that. This was as far as he had ever gone.

But he sang out, promptly, "O-kay, Dun! To the top! Let's go!" with a good spirit, gave Dunwoodie a handful of cracker crumbs, and stuffed some into his own mouth.

So Dunwoodie and his partner, Chuck and his twin, went on climbing Great Mountain, sometimes side by side, oftener single file with Chuck in the lead. They scrambled up ledges, slid back on pine needles, had the green cap snatched off by branches, climbed to retrieve it, broke the red feather, scratched their knees, split their thumbnails, sweated and panted and grunted, until finally they had left all the trees behind them. Here there was only rock with flowers blooming in all the crevices – tiny bright yellow daisies and tinier bright bluebells. The sun was close and hot, and the air swam with the spicy perfume of the flowers.

Dunwoodie was thirstier than he had ever been. He wanted to hear Chuck shout that he smelled water. Chuck wanted to smell it, too, but he didn't. All he could smell was the flowers.

"Want to rest, Dun?" asked Chuck.

"Pretty soon," croacked Dunwoodie. "Not – quite yet. Let's go – a little – farther up."

So they went a little farther. Quite a little farther. And everything was just the same. All rock, and heat, and tiny yellow daisies and tinier bluebells.

Until suddenly Chuck spied a man sitting among the flowers with his back against a rock.

Dunwoodie saw him at almost the same instant, but he put a capital letter on the word. He saw a Man.

Chuck ran toward him joyfully, but Dunwoodie hung back, not only because he had not wished to find anyone this near the top of Great Mountain but because he was afraid of the Man.

"Do you know if there's a spring near here, mister?" asked Chuck.

The Man's bare pink head was tilted back against the rock. He was looking into the clouds.

He replied in a voice that had the sound of a pipe organ, "There is a spring, but it is not very near." Then he lowered his gaze to rest first on Chuck and then on Dunwoodie, adding, "It would take many days for legs the length of yours to carry you to it."

Chuck thought the man's blue eyes, twinkling above the curly white mass of his beard, looked sorry. But Dunwoodie felt the Man's glance go through him like an electric shock, and was surprised that this was not painful. Instead, it was delightful; as if a great burst of eagerness and strength had exploded in his chest and was rushing into his nerves, and veins, and muscles.

"I don't see how we can wait that long for a drink," Chuck said. "We're pretty dry now."

He was speaking to the Man, but Dunwoodie couldn't. He threw an arm around Chuck's shoulders and spoke to Chuck.

"We can go faster," he said confidently. "You can run very fast, Chuck. And I can run as fast as you can. See if I can't."

"I should judge you are both very fast runners," said the Man. "You are good climbers, too, to have come this far up from the foot of the mountain. Are you brothers?"

"We're – twins," said Chuck, grinning broadly.

Dunwoodie found that now he, too, could speak to the Man.

He said, "We're partners."

"Yes," said the Man. "Well . . . you need not go farther thirsty. I have good spring water in my pocket."

Water in a pocket!"

The Man drew a bottle as blue as the sky from the folds of the garment of coarse gray cloth which fell loosely to just below his knees, and when he removed the stopper water bubbled out and ran in streams over his bare feet. He handed the bottle to Dunwoodie who took one swallow and passed it quickly to Chuck, for it was still spilling over and he was afraid it would soon be empty.

"Oh, ye of little faith," said the Man to Dunwoodie, smiling. "But you are a good partner to have, I can see."

He must have known what Dunwoodie was thinking!

But when Chuck had drunk deep and given the bottle back to Dunwoodie and Dunwoodie had drunk all he could and returned it to the Man it was still full, so that the stopper going in pushed a little water out. The wet side of the bottle stained the pocket where it rested.

"That's sure good water, mister," said Chuck, wiping his cool mouth on his arm.

"Than you, sir," said Dunwoodie. "Thank you very much."

"Now that you are no longer

thirsty," said the Man, "must you hurry on? Or can you rest a little here in the shade of the rock and tell me where you found such a fine cap?"

The boys sat down. chuck said Dunwoodie had given him the cap. Dunwoodie explained that it had not been a real gift, and why, which of course led to the sad tale of the savage cat, the nice little mouse, and people who permitted savagery.

"That is why we came up the mountain," said Dunwoodie. "To find a place to live by ourselves. We are going to find the high-up spring and build us a house beside it. Chuck and I would not keep a cat to catch mice."

"Ah!" said the Man. "Ah! . . . But higher up – and even here, as you can see – there is nothing of which to build a house."

Chuck had suspected that, but not wished to admit it to Dunwoodie.

"Then – where do you live, sir?" asked Dunwoodie.

"As you see. Among the rocks. I walk

between them. I lean against them. I lie upon them. The rocks of the mountain are the rooms and the furnishings of my home."

"We can do that, too."

"No. They are not yours."

"You mean," asked Chuck in awe, "you own this whole mountaintop, mister?"

"It is true that I do. But that was not the point I was making. I mean that this stony land is not your natural home. There is no shelter for you here, and you must be protected from cold and storms; you have not the proper clothing for life above the treeline. There is no proper food for you here; without it you would become ill and die. You are much too young to die. There is no work for you here, and much is waiting for you to accomplish in the countries below. Tell me more about your state."

Suddenly words poured forth from both boys so fast that they kept interrupting each other. The Man heard about all the Ryans and the Keoghs, the water which ran out of faucets, the streetlights which came on every night when it was just dark enough for them to be needed, the furnaces which began to hum when the temperature dropped, the boards Chuck's father brought home from the lumberyard, and the pastries in boxes, the rows of books on the shelves of Dunwoodie's room, the mattresses, the hot cereal on cold mornings, the ice cubes in the refrigerators on hot afternoons, the fire engines with sirens, the swimming pools, the schools, the stores, the sidewalks for rollerskating. . . .

As Chuck talked, he began to ache with wanting to see it all again.

As Dunwoodie talked, he began to think that he would not mind going back – if only the Man would go with them.

"Now describe the people of your state to me," said the Man. "Tell me how they look."

They described as well as they could the fathers who kept the stores and worked in the fields and offices and drove the trucks and buses and flew the planes and taught in the schools and doctored the sick, the mothers in the houses and the mothers who kept nursery schools and taught in the grades while other mothers worked in stores and offices and hospitals and went to meetings, and the children of their own age, and younger, and older.

"Have you ever seen the people of the other states?"

Neither of them had, of course.

"Has anyone ever described them to you?"

Dunwoodie's mother had said only that they were very different, and that someday he would see them all. Chuck had never been told anything about them, but he had overheard his father say to his mother that if she kept on having babies the older ones would have to go alone to Midway when they were ready for school there, as Midway schools were only for big kids while Two State schools were only for those under twelve.

"Still too much divided," said the Man, gazing into the clouds. "Why do they always separate themselves from those who differ from them? As one barrier falls, another rises. No two of them are alike. Why do they not glory in their variety, and build on it? When will each begin to use what is uniquely his, and to respect the best that is uniquely another's? Until they do, their destiny must hang in the balance."

The boys, not understanding what he meant, did not try to answer. They did not feel that he was really speaking to them, but both now saw sorrow in his eyes and to comfort him they crawled up beside him and knelt there, each with an arm about the other, and with their chins on his knees.

Then he looked down at them and covered both Dunwoodie's dark, curly head and Chuck's straw mop with one big, gentle hand.

"But you two," he said, "you two are partners. You are twins in a union of skills. One of you knows how to follow a trail and find water, and the other can read and write. So you will make your way safely back down the mountain, even though it will be growing dark as you go; and when you get to the foot you will make a sign and put it up to show where you have been."

It was hard to believe that there was darkness anywhere, the light was so bright all around the Man; but if he said it, the boys knew that it was so.

"It is time now for you to go."

The Man lifted their chins from his knee, and stood up. He was very tall.

"Are you coming with us?" asked Chuck, scrambling to his feet.

"Please come with us," pleaded Dunwoodie. Even on tiptoe and stretching his arm he could not now reach the hand which had lain on his head. "Please come and live with us."

"No. As this is not your natural world, yours is not mine. I have no need of what is essential to you, and find no pleasure in much that is properly pleasing to you. My place is here. But I have had great pleasure in your visit, and I shall be greatly pleased whenever the news reaches me – and news does reach me – that you are continuing to grow in courage and strength and wisdom and virtue." He raised his arm, gray folds of cloth dripping from it and leaving it bare, to point. "That is your way."

Chuck felt a faint twinge of doubt.

"It is not the way we came up," he said.

"It is your way down. Follow it."

"We will, sir," Dunwoodie said quickly, earnestly.

He took Chuck's hand and they ran a few steps. Then they stopped and looked back. The Man had not moved. He was still pointing, and the light was blinding bright all around him.

"He has nothing to shade his eyes," said Chuck.

"Nor to keep the cold winds and the snow and rain off his head," said Dunwoodie.

"Will you give him the cap?"

"It's yours now."

"Let's give it to him."

They ran back, the cap swinging between them, and held it up.

"We want to give you our cap, mister. You liked it. You said it was a fine one."

"It will shade your eyes. And keep off the wet and the cold."

The Man smiled. He lowered his arm and took the cap and turned it gently between his big hands.

"It is a fine cap," he said. "For a boy. And you are very generous. But I do not think it will fit me"

He put it on his head. The gay little green cap with the broken red feather. It was as absurd as the smallest ball from a box of Christmas decorations tossed to the top of a majestic fir tree in a forest primeval. Both boys began to laugh loudly, and the Man in the little cap joined them, his deep laughter rolling like cannonballs among the stones all the way to the peak of the mountain and back again.

Then he took off the cap and dropped it on Chuck's head.

"The people down there are looking for this," he said. "Keep it with you. I do not need it. But thank you for the laughter. I have had too little of it and heard too little of it these latter years. . . . And now farewell, my sons."

"Good-bye, sir."

"So long, mister."

They ran off in the way he had pointed, and this time did not pause or look back. It seemed to them that in some way – perhaps by his tone when he said farewell – he had told them not to.

The path along which he had sent them was smooth and plain to see. For a while a shaft of sunlight lay on it, coming from behind them and making their shadows long before. As the sunlight faded among the stunted trees, small lanterns hanging from crooked branches were lit, and continued to mark the trail through the thickening wilderness. It took far less time to go down that it had to come up. They ran all the way, and did not grow tired.

Suddenly they came to a low stone wall, and on the other side there was an open field or pasture sloping down to buildings where every window blazed with light. Against the starry sky the boys could see the outlines of cows and could hear the unmusical clank of the bells they wore around their necks.

"This must be away out in the country," Chuck said. "It may be quite a ways yet to town." He did not really mind, not being tired; but he was discovering that he was very hungry.

Dunwoodie was thinking of something else altogether.

"He said we would make a sign and put it up to show where we had been. This must be the place to do it. Here where we came out of the woods. Do you know how to make a sign, Chuck?"

"A sign is words on a board. You could make the words, I guess. I could nail the board to a tree. If we had a board for you to write on. If you had something to write with. If I had a nail. If I had a hammer."

"He said, 'When you get to the foot you will make a sign and put it up to show where you have been.'"

"We can get the stuff and come back tomorrow."

"Maybe we couldn't find the place. If it isn't marked."

"We'll push a big stone off the top of the wall. Then we'll know the place when we come to it."

But none of the stones could be moved, for they were set in cement.

"I'm hungry, Dun."

"So'm I, Chuck. But he said, when you get to the foot you will make a sign –"

Chuck sighed and climbed over the wall. Dunwoodie slowly followed him.

And there in the starlight was such a table as are in picnic areas beside superhighways. On it was set a bucket of paint, with a brush in a smaller pail beside it.

"This must be what he meant," Dunwoodie cried. "I'm to borrow this brush for a minute and paint the words on the wall."

"That's it," cried Chuck. He forgot his hunger. "Sure and that's it, Dun. What words will you put? What words?"

He wrenched the cover off the bucket and dipped in the brush, held it out wet to Dunwoodie, who did not hesitate.

He printed in bold green letters against the gray wall MAN ON MONTIN.

They did not know until he finished that a figure was coming toward them, across the field, swinging a flashlight.

Dunwoodie had just inscribed his final N when the one with the flashlight shouted triumphantly toward the lighted windows. "Found! Found! FOUND! Lost boys found! One wearing a cap with a feather!"

And then people came running and surrounded them, picked them up and kissed them, cried over them, and carried them toward the town.

II The Grammies and the Grampies

This welcome was dreamlike for Dunwoodie and Chuck, already ravenously hungry, and fast becoming sleepy. They knew the arms which carried them were not as strong or steady as their fathers' arms, but strong enough, steady enough; they knew the chairs on which they sat at table were made high with soft cushions, and that they ate their fill of thick slices of chewy bread heaped with something both tart and sweet, drank their fill of warm cocoa from big mugs. Vaguely they heard voices of a strange quality surrounding them, often coming close to them to ask, "Want Grammy to cut you another slice of bread?" and "Grammy put more applesauce and brown sugar on?" and "Grampy, you sure now that cocoa isn't too hot?" Still more vaguely they were aware of being gently undressed, guided into and out of warm, soapy water, and having big, odd-smelling garments pulled over their heads. Then they felt pillows, and a blanket being drawn up over their shoulders.

One of the deeper strange voices said, "Forgot their prayers, didn't you?"

A softer strange voice answered, "I don't know as . . ."

The last they heard was a whisper. "You're so tired tonight, honey – it's all right to say your prayers right there. If you want to."

When they woke, the sun was shining. They had kicked back the blanket and it was not a real blanket but a spread made of many little pieces of bright cloth sewn together. There was a small rug on each side of the bed, and these rugs were of bright colors braided together. The walls were covered with flowered paper, and hung with pictures of strange-looking people, mostly strange-looking children.

"You awake, Chuck?"

"I don't know. I guess so. You?"

"Mm-m. Where do you think we are?"

"I don't know. Do you?"

"No. It's somewhere else."

"The man must have told us wrong."

"What man?"

"The man on the mountain, ya nut."

Dunwoodie raised himself on his elbow.

"You remember Him, then? I was afraid I might have dreamed Him. . . . If I didn't dream Him, He didn't tell us wrong. . . . Maybe He just told us the shortest way."

"It was sure short. To here. But where's here?"

"We'd better get up and find them and ask them."

"Who?"

"The – grammies and the grampies."

"You think they know?"

"They must, mustn't they? They live here. I suppose they live here."

"Yeah! Maybe they've got more of that good stuff to eat. Wasn't that good stuff we had last night, Dun? Okay! Let's go!"

Chuck sprang out of bed. Standing on the rug he looked down at himself and let out a howl of laughter.

"Hey, Dun! What have I got on?"

"I think it's a man's shirt. A big man's shirt."

"Is that what you've got on?"

Dunwoodie climbed out of his side of the bed, stood on his rug, and looked down at himself. The cuffs of the shirts swung below their knees, and the tails of the shirts lay on the rugs, fore and aft. Dunwoodie did not laugh.

He said, "We can't get anywhere in these. Where are our clothes?... Chuck, the grammies and the grampies took our clothes! Maybe we're prisoners!"

"Not with wide-open windows, pal," said Chuck cheerfully. "Shirttails can't make prisoners out of us!"

Tails over sleeves he ran to a window.

Just then there was a knock on the door and a voice calling, "You fellas up?"

"That's a grampy," Dunwoodie whispered. "Grammies speak softer." He answered in a doubtful croak, "Well, yes – sir."

The grampy strode in and the two boys, transfixed – one all head and shirt, and the other bare from the waist down – stared at him. He bore only a faint resemblance to anything they had ever seen before when they were wide-awake, and such faint resemblance as there was was to the Man on the Mountain. His hair was on his head instead of on his face, and not curly; it stood up thick and crisp as Chuck's; but it was white. He was neither tall nor straight, but quite short and rather stooped, and he was larger around the middle than anywhere else. He did not wear a robe; he had a white shirt like those the boys were wearing (though his fitted him) and a red tie, full, dark trousers sharply creased, and shiny black pointed shoes. He was like the gnomes in Dunwoodie's storybooks, but bigger. Still he was more like the Man. This, Dunwoodie thought, was mainly because of the way he looked at you and really saw YOU – not what you were doing or what you were wearing, but YOU. Only the Man had ever looked at Dunwoodie like that.

The grampy chuckled.

"Bet you were wondering what had become of your clothes. Well, you see, they'd got pretty dirty and you'd put some holes in them, so the womenfolks washed and hung them out last night, and this morning they've been mending and ironing them. You had one pair of leather shoes between you, kind of scuffed up, and I've been polishing them a mite. So everything's ready to put on but the pair of sneakers. They're still on the line, not quite dry yet. I've got the rest here, but maybe as long as one of you will be barefooted, you'll both want to be."

Until then neither boy had noticed that he had their clothes over one arm and Dunwoodie's shoes in the other hand.

He put the heap on the bed and the shoes side by side under it.

Chuck yelped with pleasure, peeled off tails and sleeves and, leaving them in a white swirl on the floor, made a dive for his T-shirt and dungarees.

The grampy grinned at him and rested his hand for an instant on Dunwoodie's shoulder.

"You better go at it, too, son," he said. "Because looks like you have more to put on than he has. And you must both be ready for some breakfast."

From the doorway he glanced back and added, "When you're dressed, turn back your beds, pick up your nightshirts, and bring them downstairs with you. You'll see the kitchen straight ahead at the foot."

He left the door open and they could hear him going. He took slow steps.

"Your clothes smell funny?" Dunwoodie asked Chuck. "Mine do."

"Yup. That's cause of they been washed. Always smell funny right after they been washed."

"Mine's always getting washed, but they never smelled like this before. Seems as if – I know! It's the same way that thing smelled I had on last night. And the bed. The bed smelled that way, too."

"Maybe everything smells like that here. Who cares? You ready? I'm going down."

Dunwoodie was glad to have Chuck go first. He was not exactly scared, but he felt peculiar. It is one thing to wake up on the edge of Somewhere Else, and quite another to walk into it; one thing to see and hear Strange People, another to mingle with them. He had run away – it seemed a long time ago now – to escape from people, from everybody, not to be taken over by another race or clan or kind of creature or whatever the grammies and grampies were. He followed Chuck warily. He did not, he knew, want to be separated from Chuck, who bounded barefoot into Somewhere Else exactly as he had bounded up Great Mountain.

The big room at the foot of the stairs swarmed with grammies like a honeysuckle vine with bees. They were stirring with spoons and moving pots and pans about on the top of a big black block, sloshing water in a long, black trough, climbing stepladders to reach high shelves, shaking out cloths. A connecting room also swarmed with grammies scurrying back and forth between chairs and tables, running machines, rapidly working big scissors, threading needles, tying knots, or bent over setting stitches, or rocking and knitting. Some grammies were thin and some were fat, some short and some tall, but all had bright eyes, wrinkled brown faces, more or less white curly hair, thin smiling mouths, and flying hands.

One pulled out a chair for Chuck at the kitchen table, another one for Dunwoodie, more came to pile cushions on the chairs and, once the boys had scrambled up, to push the chairs closer to the table, to tuck cloth napkins inside shirt collars (this tickled, the boys ducked, the grammies laughed; their laughter was kind and their fingers soft), and then to serve breakfast. Such a breakfast! Frosty glasses of juice and crackers with raisins in them, bowls of hot cereal with dates cooked in it, scrambled eggs, bacon, cinnamon toast, and milk.

Dunwoodie, who had not thought he was hungry at all, seemed to grow hungrier with every bite. Chuck, who had waked up starving, ate as if he had not been fed for a week, and indeed he had never been fed food like this. Grammies from near and far glanced at them with delight, chattering among themselves, and beaming grampies by turns peered through the kitchen windows from the grounds outside where they were sawing limbs off trees, mowing the lawns, trimming the hedges, setting out and watering plants, cutting flowers.

"Hurry up, Dun," Chuck said at last.

Now that he had not an inch of space left to fill, he wanted to get out where those grampies were and see what they were doing.

"You boys finished?" asked the nearest grammy. "If you are, it's time for the Meeting."

"I want to go out with them," said Chuck, pointing at the grampies.

"You hear that?" a grammy asked the others. "Wasn't that always a boy all over? Feed him and he's gone wherever the men are, if he can get there."

All the grammies seemed pleased, but the nearest one said, "You can go with them when they go out again, if you want to. They're all coming in now. For the Meeting. See?"

And there they came streaming, the grammies retreating before them to throw open double doors into another big room which had many rows of folding chairs facing a big desk. The grampies nodded and grinned at the boys; some of them winked. They washed two at a time at the big black trough, dried themselves on thick white towels, combed their wet hair before small mirrors, and rolled down their shirtsleeves.

Then one grampy – the boys thought it was the same one who had brought their clothes upstairs, but could not be sure – dropped a hand on the back of each of the boys' chairs and said, "All set for the Meeting?"

"What Meeting?" Chuck asked warily.

"The one that's about to start in there. Where the womenfolks are."

"What's the Meeting for?" asked Dunwoodie. This was what Chuck must have meant to ask. A meeting is always *for* something.

"To decide what's to be done about you."

The boys exchanged quick glances.

"Gee, mister," Chuck said, "nothing's to be done about us. You've fixed us up fine. You just give me my shoes, even if they're not dry, and we'll take off. We gotta get home before dark."

"If that's what you want," the grampy said, "we'll try to arrange it. But there'll have to be a Meeting. It's farther than you think."

Chuck looked helplessly at Dunwoodie. It was getting beyond him. The grampy had sounded suddenly sad. Dunwoodie had noticed this, too.

"Well, I'll tell you what, sir," Dunwoodie said gently. "While you have your Meeting, we'll just go outside." He was thinking, "I'm sure I can find the sign the Man told me to make. Maybe we'd better go back up the mountain and find Him. I guess He wanted us to come here but we've been here. Today He'll tell us another way to go."

"Oh," said the grampy, "there can be no decision without you there. The final choice as to what is to be done about you is in your hands, of course. After you know what the possibilities and alternatives are."

Possibilitiesandalternatives. Now it was Chuck's turn to be scared, Dunwoodie's to have his first surge of confidence of the day. Dunwoodie had no idea what those words or that combination of many syllables might mean, but he knew he wanted to find out. He knew now that he liked the grampies' language and wanted to understand it and learn to speak it himself.

"It's okay, Chuck," he said. "Honest. We better go with him."

"If you say so, Dun."

"We'll go to the Meeting with you, sir."

"Good boys. You won't regret it. You'll find it very interesting."

Nobody but the Man had ever looked at them at all like that, and nobody but the Man had ever spoken to them at all like that.

The three went into the Meeting room together, and there the grampy sat between the boys with one arm across the back of each of their chairs. He was closer to them than he had ever been before, but he was not too close. He was not touching them. He had touched Dunwoodie once, briefly, when they were alone. He was not touching them here. But he was close, and that felt good.

Many other grampies and many grammies were all around, rumbling and chattering. One grampy and one grammy sat behind the big desk. When that grampy stood up and struck the desk with a wooden hammer, everyone became quiet. Then the grampy began to make a speech which he said was being broadcast all over Old State.

He said that, as they all knew, the two boys whose disappearance from Two State yesterday had been announced on the national news programs and for whose welfare they had all been so concerned had reappeared miraculously last evening in Periwinkle County, and been fed and put to bed in Harper House. Now he could add that the boys had had a good sleep, waked in good condition, and eaten a substantial breakfast. At this point a Meeting of County officials and members of the Harper House community was beginning for the purpose of learning the wishes of the boys as to the next step to be taken in their behalf, and of discussing ways and means for taking that step, whatever it proved to be.

Here the grammy reached under the desk, there was a loud click, and the grampy making the speech explained that this much of what he had to say had gone out to the national channel which would make it available for broadcast in every state of Great Country, as had his announcement the night before that the boys had arrived here safely and been welcomed as lost grandchildren should be welcomed, though this normal reception had required considerable restraint on the part of a population which had for so many years longed in vain for grandchildren.

"We know that my statement last night was broadcast nationwide, as it came in on the national news program at 11:00 P.M. exactly as I had given it. It is the first occasion on which Old State has been granted air time beyond its own boundaries. No remarks were added by the commentators. This morning on the 8:00 A.M. national news there was no reference to the boys. What the meaning is of this sudden break in information on a matter which yesterday was assumed to be of national concern we have no way of knowing. Presumably action of one kind or another is being instituted, at least in Two State, but as long as its nature remains secret from us we shall not again reveal to the national channel the exact whereabouts of these boys. Indeed, we shall not reveal it even on our own channel. Thus only those in personal contact with the boys will know where they are, and others will have no information to give if approached. However, depending on the decisions made at this Meeting, many residents of Old State may soon have the pleasure of entertaining these grandchildren. The

Meeting is now to be immediately transferred to a new location. I shall have further word for all of you on the 7:00 P.M. state broadcast."

The grammy reached under the desk and there was another click.

Dunwoodie and Chuck looked up at the grampy between them. He nodded and grinned, and then his arms came around them for an instant, drawing them up as he rose with all the others.

"What do you know?" he said. "We're going on a picnic! Great day for a picnic!"

They went outside into the sunshine where a long line of green station wagons was drawn up and grammies and grampies were climbing into them, obviously as happy to be going on a picnic as any boy could be. Other grammies and grampies were stowing boxes, bags, thermos jugs and bottles into the first car in line.

"I'm driving this one," said the grampy. "You fellas climb in the back."

Nearly hidden by boxes and bags, Chuck told Dunwoodie, "A picnic's okay. Kids can get lost easy at a picnic, if they want to. I did once I went to a picnic."

"I don't think we're going to want to."

"Not till after we eat again anyway." Chuck leered at the pile of boxes and rubbed his stomach. "I never knew eating could be so much fun."

The boys were surprised that only two of the long line of green wagons took the same turn theirs did at the end of the driveway.

"Are they going to a different picnic?" Dunwoodie asked.

The driving grampy chuckled.

"Not likely, now, is it, when we've got all the food? . . . No, you'll find we all end up at the same place. That often happens, you know, to people who start out in different directions."

"Different routes today is part of the strategy," said the grammy beside him.

Dunwoodie knew this grammy was

the one who had sat at the big desk and made the clicks. He did not know how he knew, but he did.

"What's strategy?" he asked.

"Strategy is making plans for doing what you want to do – or at least for finding out what you want to do – when you know or suspect that others are making plans to prevent your doing what you want to do, or maybe even for not giving you time to find out what you want to do."

She had turned with a bounce and was facing them as she spoke. Now Dunwoodie could see some of her differences from other grammies. Her hair was white only in front; the rest of it was red; and it was neither curly nor short but smooth and pinned into a heavy, striped knot. Her voice, though kind enough, was not soft but firm. She did not look all-giving, but as if she expected something of you. What she expected now was that you would understand what she had said.

Dunwoodie understood it very well

and was strangely elated. His leaving home had been part of just such a strategy, though he had not had a word for it. Now he had the word. He curled his bare toes in delight.

Chuck did not care about the word, but he understood enough of what she had said to ask, in some surprise, "Don't you know what you want to do?"

He thought people always knew what they wanted to do, if only they could.

"Right now, yes, of course. I want this wagon to get to the picnic grounds without being stopped, because that is where the Meeting will be resumed. I don't want the Meeting to be interrupted again. I don't yet know what I want to do after the Meeting because it depends on what takes place there. What we need now is time. Time to find out."

At the end of each of her sentences there was a small click like those she had made under the big desk, only these were not loud enough to be heard with your ears. You felt them in your head. Dunwoodie liked the feeling. It was nice. He liked the long words mixed in with the short ones. Words like strategy and interrupted and resumed.

He slid down and lay on his side, his head pillowed on his arm, watching sky and trees and the roofs of houses rush by while the beautiful words floated through his head.

"What is possibilitiesandalternatives?"

He did not know he had asked the question aloud until the grammy began to answer it.

"Possibilities are things that may happen – "

Dunwoodie raised himself quickly on his elbow to look at her, but all he saw were her straight shoulders and the striped knot of hair. She had not turned to look at him. She might have been talking to the wind. Maybe it was the wind talking. He lay down again, listening.

" – or may not. If they are good things

we work to make them into probabilities. A probability is likely to happen. The probability of something good is much better than just a possibility. But a probability is not a certainty. A certainty is something that will surely happen, so in a good thing of course a certainty is the best of all. Now, alternatives are possible choices. Since there is never more than one certainty in any one area there are no choices, no alternatives in certainty. There is usually more than one probability, and even if not there are always some possibilities clustered around it, so we have alternatives; that is, we may choose to work for either the probability or one of the possibilities, whichever we like best. Wherever there is no certainty there are always several possibilities, and therefore we have alternatives."

Click.

Dunwoodie thought he had never been so happy in his life. It seemed to him he would never again be without something to think about.

He heard from a great distance the grampy's chuckle.

"If these fellas had been to school – which I take it they haven't yet – they'd know you for a teacher, Grace."

"I doubt that. If there are my kind of teachers left back there, they've all been out of a job for years. Must have been, or we'd see something very different from the stuff on the national network. For instance, long before I left, everybody was being taught that there were no certainties. I said then there certainly were, and one of them was that they were spawning by far the most ignorant and helpless generation of so-called educated people any civilization ever had. Don't forget it was a long time ago you went to school, George."

"Didn't go far when I did," chuckled the grampy. "Left as soon as I could. When I was fifteen. Went to work in a garage. Couple of years after that I was in the Navy."

"You stayed long enough to find out, in those days, what possibilities and alternatives are."

"Maybe I couldn't tell it as smart as you did. But I can sure spell them.

POS-SI-BIL-I-TIES and
AL-TER-NA-TIVES."

"One hundred percent, George," said the grammy proudly. "You may be team captain at the Friday match."

They fell silent.

Chuck, lying beside Dunwoodie, had been thinking too.

He asked, "Don't we get to eat?"

"What did you say?" the grammy responded.

"I said, don't we get to eat."

"Of course. Whoever had a picnic without eating? What else would we do with all that's in those boxes and bags you're guarding?"

"But you said – soon as we got there – the Meeting would be – would be – "

"Resumed," said Dunwoodie.

"Good for you, Dunwoodie!" exclaimed the grammy, proudly.

Dunwoodie curled his toes.

"Chuck, my boy," said the grampy,

"the Meeting will be resumed, but if you and I can't eat and meet at the same time, we're not the men I think we are."

Chuck grinned at the back of the grampy's white head.

A few minutes later Dunwoodie sat up suddenly. A question had just come to him. Exactly the right question to ask the grammy next.

"What is the name of this country?"

The grammy turned at that.

"Great Country, of course. You have always been in Great Country. You were born in one of the four states of Great Country. Do you have any older brothers or sisters?"

"No."

"The lucky bum," said Chuck.

The grampy chuckled.

"Then you may have been born in New State, Dunwoodie. But, if so, soon you went to Two State, because that is where parents go to live with their babies. Yesterday you went climbing on Great Mountain and came down on this side of it. Great Mountain and everything around it, from sea to sea, is Great Country. It is an island. One enormous island. Nobody gets out of Great Country on his own two feet. To leave Great Country you would have to go by ship or plane. You are in the same country you have always been. But you are in a different state."

"What is the name of the state?"

"Good heavens, George," said the grammy, "hasn't anybody told the children where they are?"

"Guess not," said the grampy good-naturedly. "I haven't told them anything but to get up and get dressed and eat their breakfast and come along to the Meeting and pile into the back of this wagon. Guess it was left to you to start the geography class, Grace."

"Humph, there's a lot more to it than geography," said the grammy, "but it's as good a place as any to begin." She turned sidewise in her seat to look directly at the boys. "The name of this state is Old State. All citizens of Great Country now live first in Two State.

When they are older they go to school in Midway. Then they are moved to New State. After they have children of their own they are moved back to Two State to stay until it is time to go with the children to Midway. If they don't have children, they go to Two State anyway when they are thirty years old and stay there ten years. Then they are moved to Midway. If you think this is all very complicated, I agree with you. You don't have to remember it, but it gives you some idea of the Great Country system. What you do have to know, to understand where you are now, is that when Midway citizens get to be sixty years old they are moved to Old State. This is Old State. Everyone here is at least sixty years old, except you. Just as everyone in Two State is under thirteen or between around thirty and forty; while everyone in Midway is between thirteen and eighteen or between forty, roughly, and sixty; and everyone in New State is between eighteen and around thirty."

Chuck was blinking. The grammy gave him a quick smile and reached over to pat his hunched-up knees.

"Lost you somewhere in there, did I, Chuck? Well, a lot of other people have got lost in there, too, I can tell you."

She had not lost Dunwoodie.

"You mean they moved you here from – that other state?"

"Midway. Yes, they surely did. On my sixtieth birthday. Actually I've been told I wasn't born until five minutes before midnight, but they shipped me out on the morning plane. It was just my luck that was Evacuation Day."

"All the grammies and grampies used to live in – Midway? And before that in –"

"Before that in Two State where you came from and before that in New State, maybe, but not necessarily because – " She broke off and laughed. "Is that what you call us – the grammies and grampies?"

"That's what they were calling each other last night. I thought that was what you were."

"What we were! (George, did you hear that?) Dunwoodie, do you mean some strange kind of creature? Like you would say – oh, the giant sloths, or the elves and fairies, or the dwarfs and giants, or the prehistoric monsters? (George, I do believe they didn't think we were people. Isn't that awful?) Didn't you think we were people, Dunwoodie?"

"Well – I never thought you were monsters," Dunwoodie said earnestly.

He didn't know what else to say, but Chuck did.

Chuck said, "I think you're nicer than people."

"That's what I mean," Dunwoodie chimed in. "Nicer than people. And more fun."

"You don't just sit and read books."

"You don't just keep fixing flowers different ways."

"You don't go off driving trucks all the time, where nobody can see you."

"Or go to some office. Or to meetings

by yourselves."

"You go on picnics. And take us."

"You do all kinds of things. I don't know what yet."

"Betcha I could do the things you do."

"You've got a different – different – language. I like it. I'm going to learn it."

The grampy chuckled.

"Seems to me we're doing all right, Grace."

The grammy smiled; still her eyes had a kind of sadness in them.

"But so much to do," she said. "And so little time. . . . Now listen to me, boys. We'll soon be at the picnic grounds. Before we get there you must try to understand. We are glad you like us because we like you. But we are people. 'People' means a group of human beings, a group of persons. The people in Old State are all old, and that is the only way they are just like one another. Naturally the first thing you noticed about us is the way we are alike, just as the first thing we noticed about you was that you are two young boys. But now we know that Dunwoodie and Chuck are two very different persons, and I think you must be beginning to see that your Grampy George and your Grammy Grace are two different persons, too."

"You're both nice," said Dunwoodie.

"So are you."

"You're both fun," said Chuck.

"So are you. . . . But Grampy George is a man, and I am a woman. Once he was a boy like you. I never was, but I was a teacher so I knew a lot of boys, each one different from the others. When he lived in Two State where your home is, he had boys and girls who called him Daddy, and he worked hard all day to earn the money to keep their house warm and to buy food and clothes for them. Later, when he lived in Midway, he didn't see his children much any more because they were at school most of the time and growing up to go to live in New State, but he kept very busy. I never had any children of my own, only schoolchildren, but I saw more of Grampy George's children than he did. I kept very busy, too. All the grown people in Two State and Midway used to be very busy. I suppose they still are over there. But after evacuation to Old State nobody has to be busy. Our problem is to find ways to be busy enough. In that way we are like children. Because people who are not busy enough are not happy. And when the people of Old State are not happy they are very lonely, because they don't have families and they don't have enough work to do to keep them from thinking of how lonely they are and they don't sleep well at night and if they don't try very hard they begin to think that nobody loves them and nobody needs them and they are just waiting here to die. That is not fun at all.

"But having you come to visit us is great fun. Everybody in Old State – even those you haven't seen yet – is very happy you are here. Having you with us is the finest thing that has ever happened in Old State. We have all been waiting a long time to see our grandchildren and play with them, and teach them, even those of us who never had children of our own. In that sense, we are, as you called us, grammies and grampies. But we are people, too. The same people who once lived in Midway and maybe before that in Two State where your home is. More people come here from Midway every Friday. And the only ways we are alike is that we are all sixty years old or more, we are all your friends, we all want you to have a good time with us, and we all want you to get home safe when your visit is over."

"Are you anywhere near finished, Grace?" asked the grampy. "I'm bound to say I've driven round-and-round about as long as I can without getting dizzy-headed."

"Just one more thing," said the grammy. "Remember, boys, this man is not just a grampy. He is your Grampy George. And I'm your Grammy Grace. All the others have names of their own too, and you must learn what they are as you meet them. You can be sure they all know yours, Chuck Ryan and Dunwoodie Keogh. They all know right well that you are people, for they have known your kind of people before and even been your kind of people. That's where we have the advantage over you. Besides, there are so many of us here, and only two of you. But you are smart boys. You learn quickly."

She turned for the first time to the window and waved. Chuck and Dunwoodie looked out of the wagon, too, and saw several wagons already stopped and grammies shaking out cloths and unpacking dishes and grampies standing around smoking pipes. Grampy George blew a blast on his horn, the grammies smiled and waved cloths and dishes, the grampies grinned and waved their pipes, and Dunwoodie and Chuck scrambled to their knees and waved their arms as hard as they could.

The wagon came to a stop. Grammy Grace opened the door and sprang out. The boys, not even waiting for the tailgate to come down, scrambled over the back of her seat, and stood on bare feet in the brown pine needles, looking around in disbelief.

"What's the matter, Chuck, boy?"

"This is your Grampy Chester, Chuck –"

"Didn't you think you were ever going to get here, Dun?"

"This is your Grampy Frank, Dunwoodie – "

"You had the food and it took you so long, we didn't know but what you had stopped by the way to eat it."

"This is your Grammy Isabel, boys – "

"Well, George, you always did know the longest way round – "

"Best of that is, nobody knows where we are!"

"I do," said Dunwoodie. "I know

where we are."

"What do you mean by that, boy, – you 'know where we are'?" asked Grampy Frank, fixing him with a keen look.

"It's where we came down off the mountain last night. Where I made the sign."

Dunwoodie pointed at his words on the ledge. MAN ON MONTIN.

The grampies drew nearer.

Grampy Chester said quietly, "So it was you dipped into my paint bucket."

"I helped him," said Chuck with pride. "I took off the cover. I was the one that dipped in the brush and give it to Dun to make words with."

"Why did you do that?" asked Grampie George. "It wasn't your bucket, or your paint, or your brush."

Chuck blinked and looked at Dunwoodie. Both recognized the gently accusing note in the grampy voices, but neither of them understood it. The bucket had just been sitting there on the table. It was sitting now under a tree.

"We had to make words," said Dunwoodie.

"We didn't have anything to get out blood," said Chuck.

"It was all we had to make the words with," said Dunwoodie. "It was there to make the words."

"No. It was there to paint the table," said Grampy Chester. "We turned the table on its back and painted the legs. See? Then we turned it over to dry out. But it was heavy and turning it I got a crick in my back, so I left the paint to do the top another day. Never thought anybody would dip into my paint."

"Just a minute here," said Grammy Grace. "Why did you think you had to make words, boys?"

"He said to," said Chuck."

"He said we would. He said, 'When you get to the foot of the mountain you will make a sign and put it up to show where you have been.' I put it as high as I could reach."

"Who said, Dunwoodie?"

"The Man. The Man we found on the

mountain."

"He showed us the way down through the dark," said Chuck. "It had lanterns on trees."

"He said, 'When you get to the foot you will make a sign and put it up to show where you have been.'"

They had been talking only to Grammy Grace and watching her face. She looked very interested. But now they heard the sudden silence all around them and turned to see where it came from. The grampies had taken their pipes from their mouths. The grammies had clasped their hands. All their eyes were shining, and all their lips were smiling.

"Oh," said Grammy Isabel softly, ". . . He is still there."

"I never doubted it," said Grammy Grace shortly. "Neither did you, Isabel, and you know it. Boys, listen to me. You were right to do what the Man told you to do, of course. You couldn't have done anything else. If He told you to cross a river and there was only one boat and the man who owned the boat was not there to lend it to you, you would have to borrow it without permission. But then it would be your responsibility to try to send the boat back to its owner none the worse for having been used and to be grateful to him that he had it for you to borrow. It is a fine thing to have made the sign. However, you did use Grampy Chester's paint and brush, so now that you have explained how it happened we should find out what you can do for him in return."

"We could help him paint the top," said Chuck.

"We could help him turn over some other tables," said Dunwoodie.

Grammy Grace looked inquiringly at Grampy Chester.

Grampy Chester said, "I'll be real glad of some help when I get around to painting again. But, come to think of it, maybe not all the paint belonged to me, at that. I shouldn't wonder if enough of it belonged to the Man to paint His words."

"Good," said Grammy Grace. "The Man's will has been done. Chester contributed the paint. Chuck handed it to Dunwoodie. Dunwoodie made the words. And the boys are going to keep Grampy Chester from getting another crick in his back. Everything is in order. Let's unpack the food and start the Meeting."

Chuck and Dunwoodie thought it was a splendid Meeting. The tables were heaped with more kinds of sandwiches than they had known there were, and salads, and crackly chicken drumsticks, sweet pickles, tomatoes and apples, cookies and cupcakes, milk and fruit juices. Everybody kept pushing food toward the boys, and nobody seemed to notice how much they ate. The grampies and grammies talked a great deal and the boys understood part of it, but spoke only if asked a question. When they had eaten they climbed trees, swung from branches, ran over ledges, waving down at the talking grammies and grampies and answering the occasional inquiry tossed up to them.

The grampy who had talked in the big room was the head of the Meeting, like a president. He stood up most of the time and when the rest talked to one another instead of to him he tapped on a glass with his spoon and they talked to him again. They called him Bart. Grammy Grace sat next to him at the picnic as she had at the desk in the big room and kept writing things down.

They had thought, they said, that the arrival of two of their grandsons in Old State was a most happy accident, and their chief concern had been firstly how the boys would eventually be returned to their homes, and secondly what would be the proper time for their return, taking into consideration their wishes, their parents' wishes if revealed on the national channel, and their grandparents' wishes. Now a new element had been added to the situation by the revelation that the boys had not arrived by accident but been deliberately directed and guided to Old

State, indeed to this very spot. Therefore there was, without question, a special purpose in their being here, and an earnest effort must be made to ascertain at least in part what that purpose might be and, insofar as possible, to see that it was fulfilled.

They concluded, to begin with, that they knew of no way the boys could return home except by plane, and that they would not agree to their being picked up by a hovering helicopter as this seemed to them too risky for children of their age. Therefore, as Old State had no airports (people and supplies coming in were dropped by parachute, and Old State was also known as the Land of No Return), a landing strip would have to be built. This, the engineering grampies agreed, would take at least two weeks and require, of course, the cooperation of other states to provide the materials and machinery for the job.

The boys were asked if they would like to stay two weeks with the grammies and grampies.

Dunwoodie said, from a high branch, "Sure. Sure we would."

Chuck asked, from a higher branch, "Will you have another picnic?"

He was promised a picnic every week he was here.

He said, "We might stay a lot of weeks, I guess."

The grammies and grampies looked very pleased.

One asked cautiously, "Is it possible they could return the way they came?"

Grampy Bart said presumably they could if the way was marked but, as was plain to see, there was now nothing but the sign to show where they had emerged. It was as if the path they had followed had closed behind them.

"In case it should reopen," said a grammy in a sweeping black gown and headdress, softly, "by day or by night, I believe it would signify that the boys were to take it. And one or more of us would go with them until they were again with the Man."

"It must be a steep trail," said another. "At our ages, could we climb it?"

"I could," said the grammy in the black gown. "If the path opens, I can take the children to the Man."

It was then proposed that a watch be kept beside the painted words, around the clock, at least as long as the boys were in Old State. A schedule of hours was made, and there were nominations and elections of watchmen for the nights, watchwomen for the days.

In the meantime, it must be assumed that a landing strip would be necessary.

A committee of engineering grampies was appointed to estimate what would be required for the work, and make a list to be broadcast that evening.

A fear the grammies and grampies had been mutely wrestling with was now expressed. At any moment a strong force of young men might fly over, be dropped from the sky, take the boys, be picked up by helicopters, and disappear.

"We know we could not effectively oppose such a force," said one grampy. "Certainly if the boys' fathers were in the group we should not be justified in trying."

It was agreed that if the boys' fathers came for them, they would be welcome in Old State and their sons promptly restored to them, but that the grammies and grampies were strongly opposed to releasing the boys to strangers. Therefore every effort would continue to be made to conceal their exact whereabouts unless or until, from some hidden vantage point, they had seen and identified their fathers.

"Are we right," the boys were asked, "that you would rather stay with us until you are returned to your own families? Rather than to go away with strangers?"

Both nodded.

"My dad won't come," Chuck said. "He only goes on trucks hauling stuff."

"I don't believe mine will either," said Dunwoodie. But he was not sure.

"He's a doctor, and people are getting sick all the time."

"They'll be less likely to come," said a grammy, "if they know the boys will soon be returned. And that they are well and happy. Surely the mothers would prefer that they finish their visit properly and without risk."

"That is why the pictures must be taken and offered for broadcast," said Grammy Grace. "Boys, is it all right with you if we take some pictures of you up there?"

It made no difference to the boys. They watched the cameras being set up, then darted like squirrels among the branches, thrust grinning faces out from among the leaves, waved, wriggled their bare toes.

Grampy George said, "There, I guess you've had lunch down long enough. What say you and I go swimming?"

Swimming!

They dropped out of the tree, followed him into the station wagon, the cameras were stowed in the back, some grampies climbed in with the cameras, and they were off to the beach. It was a small beach with white sand and black rocks and the waves were small and very blue with white tops. Pointed firs grew among the rocks, and Grampy George and Chuck and Dunwoodie took off their clothes there and put on the trunks Grampy George had brought, with towels, over his arm.

"Where'd you get these to fit us?" asked Dunwoodie.

"Your grammies were making them before you were up this morning. They made you pajamas too, and other clothes. Enough to last you as long as you're here. You won't have to sleep in a man's shirt again."

That was good.

Dunwoodie said, "I didn't mind sleeping in it, but I didn't like waking up in it."

"I didn't either," said Chuck. "I didn't know what it was. But I'd almost forgot about it."

Since then there had been breakfast,

and the Meeting, and the rides, and the picnic, and tree-climbing, and now they were at the beach.

The boys ran across the white sand toward the blue waves, and the cameras whirred. Grampie George followed and the cameras stopped. But when the three were out in the water, Chuck gleefully jumping, Grampy George bent to keep a hand under Dunwoodie's stomach while he practiced strokes or under his back while he tried to float, the cameras whirred again, taking pictures of an old man frolicking with his grandsons at the shore.

That evening at 7:00 P.M., in another county, while eating supper in a big kitchen, Dunwoodie in checked pajamas and Chuck in striped saw themselves on television. There they were climbing trees, playing with Grampie George in the water, and helping to burn the picnic litter in the stone fireplace.

"Hey, look at the soot on my face," Chuck cried. "Both sides! I was awful clean when I come out of the water, but I picked up the big fork by the wrong end and got my hands all black and then I – "

"There's soot on my face too," said Dunwoodie. "You can't see it, but it's there. I know because – "

"You've got a rip in your cord pants," said Chuck. "That shows plain enough."

"We'll mend the rips as soon as the clothes are washed," said a grammy. "You have other clothes to wear tomorrow. The Periwinkle grammies made them early this morning and sent them along with you."

"Do you wash everybody's clothes every day?" asked Chuck.

"Yes, we do."

"Why?"

"Because we were brought up to think that cleanliness is next to Godliness."

"Maybe that's what makes everything smell so funny," Chuck mumbled to Dunwoodie.

"My mother washes everything every

day, too. But the clothes don't smell like these," Dunwoodie whispered.

The grampy sitting at the head of the table had sharp ears.

He said, "I shouldn't wonder if in Two State clean clothes come out of dryers. Our womenfolks hang the wash outdoors on lines. They come in smelling of salt air and pine pitch and maple sap and wild honeysuckle."

The boys thought about this, but Dunwoodie with only part of his mind.

He asked, "What's – Godliness?"

The grampies and grammies exchanged glances.

One of them said gently, "We're going to try to teach you that while you're here. It's enough for now, maybe, to say that it begins with thinking about the Man on the Mountain. While you're going to sleep tonight, think about Him."

The boys had been asleep for hours when the national broadcast came on, but every grammy and grampy who could see was watching and others who could only hear were listening. As the nationals were assembled and produced in Midway, the commentators were Midway men. The first read the initial statement received from Old State which, he said, had been read on this channel twenty-four hours before. The intervening twenty-four hours, he then said, had been a period of great anguish for the families and friends of the lost boys, and sympathetic turmoil among all adults in Two State. Films came on showing Dunwoodie's mother in a hospital bed and his father beside her in his white coat, being interviewed by the press; Chuck's mother being interviewed on her back porch from the midst of a large group of neighborhood women who had run over with their hair in multicolored curlers to bring her ice cream, cookies, frozen pizzas, and reheatable coffee, and kept interrupting her to express their own views as to what should be done; Chuck's father being interviewed at a lunch counter where he was trying to eat a hamburger and drink from a mug of coffee while surrounded by members of his union. The edict had gone out that no child be allowed beyond the walls of his house; their wondering faces separated window curtains, their astonished eyes peeped out between the slats of venetian blinds. Work had come to a standstill in Two State. The women were occupied with guarding the children as from a Pied Piper. The men paraded the streets and stormed the courthouses carrying signs demanding planes and parachutists to go Old State and bring the boys home.

The listening grammies dropped stitches in small sweaters and socks they were knitting, and the lights went out in the grampies' pipes.

However, said the commentator, cooler heads had so far prevailed. Through the night technicians had opened a new channel to Two State and beginning at 7:00 A.M. had broadcast messages at half-hour intervals all day. Statesmen, educators, and others had reminded the families and fellow-citizens of the boys that some of the people in Old State had gone there quite recently from Midway and therefore could not yet be greatly changed from what they had been while residents of Midway or from those in Midway who would soon be going there; and while this might not be so reassuring to those in Two State as to those in Midway, Two Staters must keep in mind that Midway was now the home of many who had lately been their neighbors and that others now in Two State would soon be coming to Midway. In other words, it must not be forgotten that all citizens of Great Country were human beings, separated only for greater comfort and convenience in the various stages through which all must pass. Some of those addressing the young parents of Two State even recalled that, in their childhood, visits to their grandparents had been considered by their parents not only safe but profitable, and had been peculiarly happy experiences for children. Thus it seemed wise to avoid hasty action against Old State in this emergency and to await further word on developments there. In the afternoon Midway had deemed it time to release the pictures of the Periwinkle County meeting and the announcement of the Governor of Old State relative to the condition of the boys.

Thus, gradually, the tumult had partially subsided and now a further report from Old State had been received, with pictures of the boys. There they were again, in the trees, in the water, pushing litter into the fire with long iron forks, for everyone in Great Country to see.

"It would appear," said the commentator, "that the children have no fear of the residents of Old State and regard their stay there in the nature of a holiday. Accompanying these pictures is an urgent request from Old State for immediate delivery of equipment and materials for the building of a landing strip to which we can send a plane to pick up the children and return them safely to their homes. This is being assembled and will be dispatched tomorrow. We again urge Two State to make every effort to reduce tension and return to normal life while the necessary arrangements are being made toward the end they so much desire. The special broadcasts to Two State will continue through tonight and tomorrow, but only hourly unless conditions there seem to demand half-hourly communication."

Dunwoodie and Chuck woke the next morning in a house so quiet that they could hear no sound but birdsongs, the gurgling of a brook finding its way among stones, and the rustle of the curtains at their open window. They lay for a few minutes listening and pointing out to each other the spots of color reflected from an octagonal piece of blue glass on the windowsill. When they went downstairs there was only one grammy in the kitchen and only one grampy in the yard. She called to him that breakfast was ready and the four sat down together. The grampy bent his head, and the grammy bent hers. Dunwoodie and Chuck exchanged glances and bent theirs.

"May this food be blessed to our use. In the Lord's name, we ask it. Amen," said the grampy. He raised his head, grinned at the boys, and lifted his glass of orange juice. "Drink up, fellas," he said. "There's better on beyond."

The grammy brought a platter of hotcakes and a pan of bacon from the stove, filling their plates, setting pitchers of syrup between them. One kind of syrup was the color of gold, and the other a royal purplish-red.

After a while Dunwoodie asked, "Who did you talk to when we looked at our plates?"

"I was asking the blessing of God," said the grampy.

"Who is God?"

The grampy looked at the grammy.

She said, "He is the Great Spirit. He made the world and everything that is in it. He is our Father. We love Him and trust Him and try to serve Him."

“Is He the one on the mountain?” asked Chuck.

“We cannot say as to that. You are the first people we have known who have seen the Man on the Mountain. But we have heard of others to whom He has spoken. If he is not indeed God, He must be very close to God, since He can perform miracles.”

“What is miracles?” asked Dunwoodie.

“Things none of us could do for ourselves. Mysterious things. Great and good yet very simple things.”

“Like carrying a spring in a bottle in His pocket?” asked Dunwoodie.

“And hanging lights just by pointing His finger?” asked Chuck.

“Things like that,” nodded the grampy.

“And like sending you to us for a little while,” said the grammy, touching the nearest elbow of each of the boys.

“What is blessing?” asked Dunwoodie.

“God’s blessing shows us what is

right and what is wrong. It teaches us the best way to express our love for one another. It makes us stronger and wiser and more useful."

"Won't God bless us if we don't ask Him?"

"All we know is that the asking helps us. We are stronger and feel wiser and more sure of what we should do and be as soon as we have asked."

"I never heard anybody ask before."

"But now you have, and wherever you are you can ask."

After breakfast the boys went out with the grampy and shook the soil off the squares of grass he turned over with his spade, dug into the ground with their hands as he showed them, making a soft bed for new plants he brought out of the shed in boxes. As they worked he told them how in olden days, before the separation of the states into age groups, this had been a farm and whole families had lived together on it all their lives. A whole family, he explained, had not only young children and their mothers and fathers in it, but older children and grandparents and maybe a uncle or an aunt. There were beds for all of them under the same roof and a big table where they ate all their meals together, and maybe a big fireplace or a big stove that they sat around on cold evenings and popped corn or peeled and strung apples; or maybe the women sewed and the men mended harnesses and the children studied their lessons. Sometimes people told stories, or somebody read aloud from a book. On warm evenings they sat out in the yard to do these things and often their neighbors came over, bringing their work.

Once that had been the way nearly everybody lived in all the states, the grampy said. But then the cities began to grow, and many young people, when they were old enough and thought they had learned all they could at the little country school down the sandy road, moved into the cities to learn different kinds of things and to do other kinds of work than farming. But the old people mostly stayed where they had been and some young people did too, and those who went off to the cities could always come back to visit and often did. The old people visited their young in the cities, too, and sometimes went to live with them during their last years, and the young people grew older and had both young and older children living with them even in the cities. So, when Great Country divided the states as they were divided now, this was the way of life the older people, especially, remembered happily and wanted to keep. Since they could no longer live with other generations, they had tried to make family units of those sent to Old State. One way of doing this had been to preserve all the best of the big old houses here just as they had been, and make them the headquarters of perhaps two hundred citizens each, who took turns living in them and who, when not living in them, could go there whenever they wished to eat together, or work together, or have a meeting, or spend a night.

"Harper House, where you went first," said the grampy, "is one of them. This is another. We wanted you to stay in these old family houses so that you will know what they are like. I don't know how much longer they'll be here, for the people coming in from Midway seem more satisfied than the first ones were with the little houses the government sends in the first week of every year and drops down in an empty space." He seemed now to be talking to himself. "I suppose they're more what they're used to. Handy as all get-out. About all anybody has to do is press a button. But they don't seem any more like home to me than a raft." He sighed, then picked up his spade and brightened. "Oh, well, there's still a lot of folks that feel the same as I do. I guess now we've got just about enough time to tidy up before Grammy Helen has our lunch ready. I hear her setting the table on the porch."

There were blue bowls and mugs on a yellow cloth, yellow roses climbing the screen and bees buzzing in them, a wooden bowl of apples, bananas, purple plums, and kumquats, and the watermelon smell of fresh-cut lawn grass drying in the sun.

They had scarcely finished eating when grammies and grampies began coming from all directions.

"Hear the planes?" they called. "They're just back of the mountain! Come on, boys! You'll want to see the drop. This ought to be a big one."

"Yes, run along," said Grammy Helen. "I'll come soon as I have the dishes in to soak."

The boys ran off to join the parade climbing a hill from which everybody watched the big planes circling over the valley and dropping bags, cartons, and shiny machinery which floated down as if they had no weight but threw up clouds of dust when they landed.

"Get up this tree, boys," said somebody suddenly. "Get up there quick and wave your hat."

The green hat with the red feather was thrust into Chuck's pocket, and a few minutes later both boys were sitting on a high branch, waving the hat by turns.

"Do they see us?" Dunwoodie called down. "Do they see us?"

"We have no way of knowing," a grampy answered.

A grammy said, "We always used to wave during the drops, but there was never any sign they noticed. So we stopped. Almost seems as if there is nobody in those planes. But I suppose there still must be. Though folks coming in see nobody but one another after they leave Midway until they land."

As the planes disappeared around the mountain, everybody hurried into the valley, some to open the new containers and others to set up the machinery with little power-driven tools which worked like magic, while others measured and planned the course of the airstrip to be built. It was not nearly as interesting to the boys as making a garden bed and setting out plants. They soon began to feel thirsty and then sleepy.

"I've got a jug of lemonade in my car," said a grampy who had driven over from Somewhere Else.

"Bring it up here in the shade," said a grammy.

The boys drank deep and stretched out on the moss. Grammies spread aprons to sit on and pulled the boys' heads to their knees, gently lifted locks of hair to let in the breeze, and began to sing lullabies.

"Sleep, my child – " . . . "Once there was a little bird – " . . . "Out on the water in my gondola, list to the mockingbird saying 'I love you' – "

On the national channel that night there were pictures of the airdrop, of the boys working in the garden, and of the boys asleep and the grammies singing. There were also pictures of Dunwoodie's father helping his wife from the car as she returned home from the hospital. She asked anxiously as to what was known of the supply in Old State of drugs suitable for children, especially tetanus antitoxin and snakebite serum, since the boys were outside so much and running about barefoot, and gave the trade name and amount of the vitamins Dunwoodie should have daily. Chuck's mother had made herself unavailable for comment by locking her doors and refusing to answer the telephone, but the restrictions on children had been lifted and small Ryans drawing chalk pictures on the sidewalk said, "She's okay. She's readin'. They brought her a whole stack of new books." Bob Ryan's truck was flagged down on the highway and he leaned out of the cab to shout, "Never thought a six-year-old kid of mine would get on his own two feet to where they had to build an airstrip to get him out. How about that, huh?" There were other pictures of streets, schools, and offices in Two State, indicating that life there was returning to normal, and the young Governor of Two State in his news conference stated that his people were far from as flappable as they may have at first appeared and as Midway seemed to assume, that only the daily assurances of the boys' well-being and rapid progress on the Old State airstrip were now of interest to Two Staters, and that the barrage of messages from Midway must cease as they were neither needed nor desired and would not be broadcast if recevied over the special channel.

"But let Midway make no mistake," warned the young Governor. "Since they have the planes, it is their responsibility to return these boys to us at the earliest possible moment. Otherwise, the Midwayans will find that Two Staters are not by any means helpless and will not remain at their mercy. We have our own means of getting our boys, if need be, and, if it comes to that, effective retaliation will be taken against those who have failed in their duty to us in this extraordinary emergency."

The middle-aged Governor of Midway, asked for his reaction to this warning, smiled wryly and said, "The Boy Wonder of Two State does not sound exactly unflappable to me. However, it is well that he indicates he is willing to hold his fire for a reasonable length of time, especially since to the best of my knowledge he has none beyond the heat of his own breath. In case what he has in mind is hijacking a delivery plane, I have directed that no deliveries be made in Two State until further notice. The Boy Wonder speaks of our duty to his state and its problems, but you will note he seems unaware that it has any to us. Naturally this comes as no surprise. Midwayans have become accustomed to receiving nothing but demands from all sides. A word of appreciation for our services might be such a shock as to incapacitate us all, which of course is the situation the other states wish above all to avoid. Do they ever consider the possibility, do you suppose, that we may one day, to a man and a woman, quietly choose to stop? Stop running, stop producing, stop delivering?"

All over Old State grammies and grampies exchanged glances. They had been citizens of Midway not very long ago.

"In the meantime," said the Midway Governor, rising from his desk and stuffing papers into his attaché case, "we shall send a rescue plane to Old State as soon as it can land, and return the boys to their parents."

The lovely days swam by. Each night on the national channel there were assurances of adequate medical supplies in Old State – and no call upon them from the boys – and reports that no poisonous snakes had survived the onslaught of the first citizens to settle there after it was set up; that Dunwoodie and Chuck were moving freely about the state, but always under the watchful eye of grandparents, having experiences they enjoyed, learning new skills, eating well, sleeping well, gaining in self-confidence, and becoming very helpful. Pictures were shown of them at these pursuits, with grandparents in the background. Pictures were shown, too, of the progress of the airstrip.

"This progress may seem slow to our fellow-citizens," said the Governor of Old State (whom the boys knew as Grampy Bart), appearing unexpectedly on the national channel, the first time an Old Stater had spoken from the screen, "but it must be remembered that we who are here are all old men. We are working as fast as we can, commensurate with the care we are determined upon to be certain that what is called the rescue plane will land and take off without incident. We estimated that the work would take us two weeks, and that seems to have been about right."

Finally one hot night, long after grampies had let the boys run without clothes through a warm rain to swim in a dark pool, and brought them home, and grammies had heard their prayers and tucked them in bed, all over Old State people gathered before their television screens to find out whether their latest message had been a bombshell to the rest of Great Country.

That morning, along with the pictures of the boys and of the completed landing strip, the Governor of Old State had announced to the national network that all was now in readiness for the rescue plane and that its arrival would be expected the following day. However, regardless of who flew the plane or who were its passengers, the boys would not be allowed to board it unless accompanied by two citizens of Old State who had been elected to accompany them.

"We wish," said Grampy Bart, "not only to receive here a direct, personal account of the arrival of our grandsons at their own homes, but also to see for ourselves – or to hear from a point of view we can understand – what life is like now in Two State, where these children who are very dear to us are growing up; and also to make a survey of Midway and New State. We wish our representatives to travel throughout Great Country and bring back a report on conditions. We ask that transportation from state to state, and hospitality in each, be assured our representatives. We feel that we have earned this courtesy. We have grown weary of being imprisoned. The landing strip is ready. The rescue plane may land here tomorrow. But unless it carries our representatives when it takes off it will not carry our grandsons."

As the days had run into weeks and the patient watchmen at the picnic area where the boys had come off Great Mountain had seen the foliage behind their sign only grow thicker and more interlaced, it had slowly been borne in upon Old Staters that the purpose of the miracle which had sent the boys here must be to bring down the barriers now separating the generations. A miracle had brought the very young and the old together. Now they, by strong and determined effort, must take the next steps.

The grammies could not knit as they awaited the response to their Governor's ultimatum. The grampies could not smoke. They sat with hands clasped as in prayer, and indeed many of them were praying, eyes fixed on the blank screen and ears assailed by the hum of empty airwaves.

Suddenly the face of the Governor of Midway flashed on.

"My fellow-countrymen," he began, "together with my Council in extraordinary session I have tonight made a decision of considerable importance to many of us and perhaps to all of us. Though it is impossible to say in advance what the outcome will be, this government is moving in a direction it firmly believes is against any belligerent confrontation. Peace being desired above all things by the citizens of all states of Great Country under usual conditions, recent events have been most unusual, and throughout this day we have been on the brink of civil war, a crisis which could not continue, a threat which must not prevail, a challenge which had to be faced, a conflict of wills on which this government is obliged to sit in judgment.

"I beg you to listen to me carefully.

"Most of you will recall that some weeks ago two small boys who wandered away from their Two State homes by some means not at all understood by any of us reached Old State from which it has been impossible to recover them peacefully without the cooperation of our citizens who live there. The cooperation Old Staters offered was the building of an airstrip (materials and equipment to be provided by this government) where a plane could land to pick up the boys. We prevailed on Two State, though naturally impatient, to accept this delay in view of its apparent maximum safety for their boys. This morning the Governor of Old State announced that the strip is completed and the rescue plane may land there tomorrow.

"However, he has now set a new condition on which the boarding of this plane by the boys is contingent. They are being kept in hiding and will not be brought forth unless two elected representatives of Old State are permitted to fly to Two State with them and are assured of safe passage not only from Old State to Two State but on a circular flight around Great Mountain and stopovers of a few days in each of their neighbor states.

"As soon as this message reached Midway it was conveyed to me and shortly thereafter I sent it on to the Governor of Two State, who replied within the hour that his people demanded the use of enough planes to fly several hundred volunteers into Old State at daybreak tomorrow to find the boys and bring them home. He was advised to reconsider this demand as, if we acceded to it, it might well result in violence. He replied that no weapons would be issued to these volunteers; therefore, since only the government has weapons, there could be no violence. 'The Old Staters will be told to stand aside while our search is conducted,' said he. 'If they do as they are told, they will not be hurt.' He was asked, 'But if they do not stand aside? Old people can be very stubborn.' His reply was to the effect that Two Staters had had enough of nonsense, and wanted planes in which to go after the boys; he implied that by one means or another they would get them, all others states lacking either the physical strength or the determination, or both, to match those of his people when aroused as they are now.

"My Council came together with me immediately and remained in session until an hour ago. The maintenance of cool heads was absolutely essential. The citizens of Two State are, in the vast majority, the parents of young children, and all of us have felt with them through these days of acute uneasiness as to the whereabouts and welfare of two of their treasured charges. However, Old State has gone to some length to carry well, apparently, their responsibility for those boys whom they call their grandsons, and to reassure the children's parents and friends that they were safe and happy. Now both states have made a demand on my government and it was the conclusion of my Council that we would be wise to respond to both, but in order of difficulty and degree of danger to the security of the country.

"Accordingly, an hour ago I broadcast to Two State my decision to send the rescue plane to Old State in the morning with six secret servicemen aboard. This plane and these men are scheduled to land at our Air Force base in Two State at noon precisely, and Dunwoodie Keogh and Charlie Ryan to run down the ramp in excellent health and spirits to their parents who, we assume, will be at the foot of it. I further informed Governor Hurd that if this mission has not been accomplished at the hour set, six transport planes, each equipped to carry nearly a hundred men, will take off from Carson AFB here and be at his disposal within an hour for such use as he and his advisers deem necessary.

"Governor Hurd's response has just come in and I give it to you as received."

The face of the Governor of Midway was replaced on the screen by the figure of Governor Hurd in the doorway of his State House. He was ringed by microphones. His face was cold. His stance was angry. His voice was surly.

He said, "I have prevailed upon my people to make this one further concession, and I commend them for their restraint. It is the last I shall ask of them in this matter. The absolute last. If that plane does not return the boys in good condition at noon tomorrow and the transport planes are not delivered by 1:00 P.M., we shall move in on Old State (and shortly thereafter on Midway) in a manner which will doubtless surprise them and with an effectiveness that will appall them. They have all forgotten, apparently, the strength in the hands of outraged young men. They have caused us great suffering, they have denied us our rights, the Governor of Midway has insulted us, and now they expect us to trust them. Let me make it clear that we no longer trust anyone but ourselves. We delay our action until noon tomorrow only because we cannot be ready for action on our own sooner than that. And I add this fair warning – we give no assurances to anybody from outside our state of safe stopovers in it, whether they come out of curiosity or for other reasons. Two State does not want Old Staters here. We only want our boys back. When we have them, we shall proceed to forget, as before, that Old State exists, and to the end that we shall never again be reminded we demand that Midway – which takes our taxes and controls what they buy – build a high wall across our section of the base of Great Mountain. Until that wall is built, Midway will get no more tax money from Two State. . . . To my own people I say, 'Goodnight and sleep well. Tomorrow we begin making history.'"

Young Governor Hurd vanished. Middle-aged Governor Wireman reappeared, looking very tired.

"I now address myself to Old State. It is as it has always been the wish and the policy of my government to protect you. We found you a pleasant place, we finance your every need and reasonable desire, we go to great lengths to keep you beyond the reach of attack. But you are now in a position to make this protection very difficult, and that is what you are doing. You call it imprisonment. We in Midway cannot understand your attitude. You have what we in Midway dream of one day achieving. I beg of you to appreciate it, cherish it, help us to maintain it.

"To spare you possible invasion, the permission you asked is granted for two of you to board the rescue plane with the boys tomorrow morning, but surely you will behave rationally and decide against it if only for your own safety. Much as my government might like to, we are far from able to assure you of a friendly reception beyond your own boundaries. Indeed, it appears that anywhere else you would be in constant danger. I can only say that the secret servicemen assigned to this plane will do all in their power, if you board it, to see that you are taken where you want to go, protected while you are there, and returned to your own state as soon as you choose to go. In any case, that must be within a week at the most, as a week is the limit of their tour of duty on this mission which would be as dangerous for them as for you.

"Again I make an urgent plea to Governor Barton and all citizens of Old State. Put the boys on the rescue plane in the morning, and remain where you are. Have a quiet, leisurely lunch and a long afternoon nap. I only wish I could join you in both, but that is impossible for me for another ten years. Believe me, you are the most fortunate of us all."

The screen went blank. Grampy Bart snapped off the humming.

"Well, what do you say, George?" he asked. "Grace?"

Grampy George drawled, "Looks like I'd better get along to bed, so I'll be up in time to shave before breakfast. Ain't in the habit of doing it till afterwards, late years."

"Then don't forget to pack your razor," Grammy Grace reminded him. She added comfortably. "I've had everything I need in my suitcase for three days, except what I always carry in my handbag. The worst thing would be if I went off without my reading glasses. Chuck asked me the other day, 'Why can't you read with your eyes, Grammy?'"

III The Mommies and the Daddies

The Rescue touched down at Two State Air Force base at 11:57 A.M., Two State time. It was the first plane to land in Two State in two weeks, and the roar of its approach had seemed thunderous in the unaccustomed air. Except for parked and quietly cruising fire trucks, ambulances, and police cars, the field was completely empty. As The Rescue's engines were cut off, the trucks and ambulances which had been moving stopped in line with others at the edge of the field, while the police cars, filled with officers, quietly formed a circle around the plane. It was a sunny, humid, windless noon in Two State, and now the silence was as oppressive as the weather.

As the ramp came down and the plane door opened, the iron gates of the Port Facility swung outward to permit the passage of a dozen policemen surrounding a small, dark man and woman, and clanged shut again in the faces of several thousand young parents. As the foot of the ramp the police detail surrounded the couple as the crowded police cars surrounded the plane. Two burly secret servicemen preceded the boys down the ramp. Two more followed them. The third pair remained at the top, filling the doorway.

Grammy Grace had moved over to the window seat which Dunwoodie had occupied beside hers and was on her knees there, her forehead pressed against the glass.

"Look to you, George, as if Two Staters have maximum security?"

"Against any harm they think we could do 'em, any way," Grampy George agreed from where Chuck had been sitting beside him. "Now I think of it, though, seems funny nobody locked them blasted belts onto us. . . . Must say them young policemen look tough."

"Tough – and handsome," said

Grammy Grace. "And deadset on doing their duty. . . . There, those people are Dunwoodie's parents. I thought they must be. And he is glad to see them. That's a relief. He didn't know whether he would be or not. He was uneasy the whole trip."

One of the policemen was rolling a newsreel camera as had been promised the Two State press, this being the only sure means of keeping its representatives off the field.

If the small, dark man and woman had not been Dunwoodie's parents, he might have turned on the ramp and tried to duck back between the secret servicemen's legs. But as soon as he saw Kennedy and Carmel Keogh he was swept by happy excitement, cried, "Hi, Mommy! Hi, Daddy!" and went running toward them as fast as he could go. His mommy stooped to hug him, crying too much to say anything but, "Oh, Dunwoodie – Dunwoodie – Dunwoodie. . . ." His daddy picked him up, tossed him in the air, caught him when he came down, and said huskily, "Why, – I think you've grown, son! You're hard as a – as a nutshell! WHAT kind of clothes are these you have on? And isn't that other boy wearing your hat?"

Of course Grammy Grace and Grampy George could not hear a word that was being said, but they did not have to hear; they could see that Dunwoodie was getting a royal welcome. Still Grammy Grace was worried.

"You suppose there isn't anybody here to meet Chuck?"

Grampy George chuckled.

"Chuck didn't figure his folks would be here, and it didn't bother him a mite. He's used to making out on his own. Look at him now, Grace!"

One of the policemen had bent down to explain to Chuck that his mommy had not been able to come to the airport because she was in the hospital for a few days with his brand-new baby sister; and his daddy could not come because he was at home with the Ryan children who were too young even to go to nursery school, but...

Chuck, not half-listening to the explanations, had interrupted to say, "You're a cop, I betcha. You're all cops, I guess. I didn't know there was so many cops. I never saw more than two at once before. You having a picnic or sumpen?"

The officer who had been talking to him laughed, and so did all the others who were near Chuck. They stood laughing with their feet wide apart and their big arms folded across their broad chests. Chuck's feet edged apart, his small arms crossed each other across his narrow chest, and he laughed too, his face turned up.

"Some picnic!" roared one of the officers. "Some chase you've led us, Chuck, boy."

"Oh, what the heck," said another. "If it wasn't this it would be something else."

They were all beaming down at

Chuck.

Chuck asked, "Hey, can I be a cop?"

"You sure can, fella," said one. "It'll take a few years' growth, but you can start practicing right now."

He pulled off the featherless hat Chuck was wearing, tucked it into Chuck's pocket, dropped his own cap on Chuck's head, swung the boy to his shoulders, and started jogging toward the iron gates, one of Chuck's ankles in each of his big hands.

But suddenly there was an outcry from Dunwoodie who, between his mommy and his daddy, had been moving slowly away from the plane, talking very fast to explain his clothes and why Chuck was wearing his hat, and finding that the branches of his story led in a dozen different directions. Then he had tried to stand still, looking around in bewilderment, asking where Grampy George and Grammy Grace were; but his mommy only hurried him along faster, drawing him by his hand in hers, his daddy propelling him ahead by a hand on his shoulder until in desperation he tried to pull away from them and howled, "Chuck! CHUCK! They're leaving them! They're leaving them! Grammy Grace! And Grampy George!"

At that Chuck let go of the policeman's ears and looked behind him; looked at the widening empty space between him and the ring of police cars inside which the secret servicemen stood, two at the foot of the ramp, two halfway up the ramp, and two in the plane door.

"Hey, wait!" he shouted, struggling to get down. "We've got to go back and get Grampy George and Grammy Grace –"

But the policeman did not let Chuck down, and Dunwoodie's daddy picked him up. The Two State iron gates opened, the prodigal boys were carried through, and the gates closed.

The plane's two passengers heard nothing, but saw it all.

The secret serviceman loomed at the

front of the cabin and said stiffly, "Since the return of the boys has been accomplished and since it must be obvious to you, sir and madame, that Two State will not admit you, I trust you will now permit us to fly you home."

"Certainly not," said Grammy Grace. "Old State has kept its agreement. Now the rest of the country will keep its or be very sorry. Exceedingly sorry."

"I suppose that is a threat," said the secret serviceman, coldly. "Are you implying that if you are not granted admission to other states, you will use some sort of ancient magic to entice more of our children away from their parents?"

"Oh, what blasted nonsense," exploded Grampy George. "Ancient magic!"

"Probably he can't help it, George. Probably they call anything they don't understand 'ancient magic,'" said Grammy Grace. "Never mind what I am 'implying,' young man. Just pay attention to what I say. We were promised hospitality in our neighbor states, and –"

"Not by the government of Two State, you weren't. So if you're too stubborn to go home, we'll take off for Midway and find out there what to do with you."

"You're taking off for nowhere for at least three days unless other accommodations are provided for us here," said Grammy Grace. "We've made our plans to remain in Two State that long, and that long we may remain. This is a poor roof to have over our heads but better than none."

"You are determined to stay in the middle of this airfield for three days?"

"Bound and determined," said Grampy George, "if that's as near as we can get to them boys they just carried through them gates. 'Course I'll have to get out and walk around the plane now and again. I feel a cramp coming on in my left thigh a'ready."

"You can walk in the aisle."

‘I’ll walk on the ground,” said Grampy George. “If anybody tries to stop me from getting even a breath of air here, I’ll have a pretty story to tell when I get to Midway.”

“Alighting will be impossible. Delivery planes will be landing, unloading, and taking off every few minutes all afternoon. No supplies have come into Two State for two weeks, as the result of this crisis.”

“The result of Two State’s reaction to what you call a crisis,” said Grammy Grace.

“Nevertheless, if you’ve got an objection to having those planes run down an old man trying to stretch his game leg,” said Grampy George, “you’d better get us somewhere where it’s safe to stretch. Cramp’s run down and tied a knot under my knee.”

“What in blazes is a cramp?” asked another secret serviceman curiously. He had come up the aisle to listen to what was being said.

“You’ll know when you get one,”

said Grampy George. "And get 'em you will when you're old as I am, likely."

"Long before then we shall have stopped the aging process," said Number One.

"By decree?" asked Grammy Grace.

"By medical treatment, of course."

"Take care you don't stop the learning process at the same time."

"On the contrary. It is well known that age makes learning impossible."

"It can. So can a lot of other things. Closed minds, for instance."

"We'll take our chances," grinned Number Two. "Long as we don't get gray hair and cramps and – such like."

"Well, I've already got 'em all," said Grampy George, "and if you don't let me out of here pretty quick I'm going through a window."

Following an exasperated sound, Number One said, "I will buzz Midway for orders."

As he went down the aisle, Grammy Grace called after him, "You going to do away with death, too?"

"Eventually, no doubt," he answered without turning.

"And right after that, naturally, you'll do away with having children. Or else there'll soon be pyramids of people standing on one another's shoulders all over Great Country. Best to leave alone a system you can't improve on, I always thought."

But nobody was listening, not even Grampy George. He was really in agony.

A wrangle had started in the tail. Grammy Grace gathered that another secret serviceman was already talking with Midway. Number One first tried to interrupt and then to get hold of the receiver but apparently had neither higher rank nor greater strength than the man in possession of it. After a couple of minutes of loud talk and shuffling, the man on the wire shouted:

"I have your orders and shall proceed as agreed. Direct all planes to circle until Ace has The Rescue in the hangar. Roddy will go with me in my car. I'll report to you immediately upon arrival. Now here's Spike, the sickening sadist. What you ever put him on this mission for –"

The tallest, thinnest, darkest-complexioned secret serviceman came striding up the aisle, suitcase in one hand, and all but carried Grampy George out of The Rescue and down the ramp. The shortest, fattest, blondest one was close behind with the other suitcase and Grammy Grace, who had no more firsthand (or knee) knowledge than he did of what a cramp felt like and needed no help to keep up with him. A minute or two later the four were in a car, a gate was being raised, and they were shooting under it, the two travelers from Old State in the back seat and Long and Short in the front.

"I hope to my soul, George," whispered Grammy Grace, "your knee is so you can get your mind off it and take note of where we are."

"It's loosening up now. Where in tarnation are we?"

"Two State, of course. But not in it. Nothing's in it. Did you ever see such a place in your life?"

"Looks to me like they'd put all the inside outside and took all the outside inside."

"Only there's no inside."

All buildings, even commercial buildings, were entirely of glass and transparent plastic, with sliding walls, and none had more than one story. To find space for so many the buildings had walls in common or at most only the width of a walk between them. Narrow strips of lawn with buildings on one side and a street on the other were otherwise without boundaries and crisscrossed the state like basketry.

"No place to start and no place to stop, looks to me."

"No place to hide. Looks like a cake that never rose but somehow got flopped whole out of the pan."

"No wonder Chuck and Dun took to the mountain."

"Wonder to me they don't all. . .

Been a big change since I used to visit my Aunt Abbie here when I was little."

"I used to live here, you know."

Most of Two State was flat but there were occasional low hills, and just over the crest of one the car darted behind a square block of what looked like masonry.

"Is that – stonework?" Grampy George asked, blinking.

"Yup," said Short. He and Long had turned in their seat and were grinning at the Old Staters.

"I had a brainstorm," said Long, "about the time you started arguing with Spike. Couldn't see how you could be kept on The Rescue in any comfort at all. Made no sense. All that was needed was for Two Staters to be separate from you and you from them. So I asked Roddy why you couldn't use his pad. If he was willing, it seemed to me like the ideal solution."

"And I said sure," Short chimed in. "Nobody here. My wife and I don't have any kids. Wife's at work. I'll call her there and tell her to go to Max's place tonight to stay with his wife. That is, if you want to stay here after you look it over. Midway says it's okay."

"Can I get back on the ground?" asked Grampy George.

"Out you come," said Long.

He opened the car door, helped Grampy George down, and kept a hand under his elbow as he began to move about.

"Have to ask you to wait there, ma'am," Long said to Grammy Grace. "Just until Roddy gets the gate locked. Then you'll both be free as – as –"

"Two birds in a cage?" asked Grammy Grace, peering around.

It seemed that what the car had been driven into was a kind of courtyard a hundred feet square, more or less, thinly grassed over but with bare patches and the grass uncut. This was bounded on three sides by well-built, cut stone walls some ten feet high, and on the fourth by one side of the square lock which was about the same height and by the closely barred iron gate Short was now closing (it creaked) and locking (it grated).

"That's about it," Long answered, grinning. "Better than The Rescue, or handcuffs and balls and chains. Or isn't it?"

"Having had no experience with the restrictions of handcuffs, balls and chains, or small cages," said Grammy Grace, "I must reserve judgment, but presume you are right. Life in a plane is certainly as near to being not worth living as I can imagine. I put it at the absolute bottom of my list. . . . You and your wife actually live here?"

She was asking Short, who had come back from securing the gate and was opening the car door on her side.

"In a manner of speaking. I guess it's more that we meet here when our hours off coincide. It seems to suit us – while it lasts. Come on in and look around."

Grampy George was walking more easily, like a sailor finding his landlegs. Long had let go of his arm. They were strolling as any two men might who have nowhere in particular to go, and Long was answering Grampy George's questions. It was said that this had once been a churchyard, and one reason the space was still clear was that Widget Chase the Fourth had been buried here. Widget Chase the Fourth, of course, was the Senator who had authored the constitutional change which brought about the present division of Great Country. When he was assassinated a few months later, at the age of thirty-one, the government had impulsively put up a great shaft here as a monument to him.

"I recall reading about it in the papers," said Grampy George. "Happened not long after I went to Midway. Heard the assassin was one that didn't want to move. I couldn't help feeling with him some at the time, and still do. See, I grew up in this part of the country. Lived here all my life until I got sent to Midway. No telling now, I guess, where our place was. All seems to look as good deal alike."

Long responded that it was a great mistake to get attached to a place. For instance, Roddy and Jan were foolish to hang on to this spot just because it was different from anywhere else. Every day they stayed was only going to make it harder for them to leave, and it was literally coming down around their ears. But it was certainly useful right now.

"What become of the shaft you were telling about? Don't seem to be here."

Long said no, there was no space to spare for such things in Two State; the time was coming when neighboring states would have to cede some of their land to Two. As building lots were laid out in his direction, the church – which hadn't been used for a long time – had been taken over as a recreation hall and the small churchyard stones had been hauled away to clear a playground for children where they could be left while their mothers were inside. But as the houses came nearer and the population grew, the building and the playground became increasingly inadequate and impractical for the purpose. Two State had notified Midway that both shaft and building were coming down. Midway would have liked to move the shaft to the Government Center there, but could figure out no way to do it, so finally it had been taken down, broken up, and put into roadbeds. Soon after that the roof was removed from the building. The steeple and belfry (Long could not remember the names for these appurtenances but Grampy George filled them in) were already gone, having rotted from lack of paint and become unsafe. When Roddy got his appointment to the service, Midway had asked that, during the shortage of housing, he and Jan be allowed to have headquarters temporarily in the basement apartment. This was possible because, it was said, the minister who started this church had begun by building the foundation, with what help he could get, and it was roofed and finished off, complete enough so that church meetings had been held in it for several years.

"Why, that was Elder Walmsley," said Grampy George. "He was before my time but I remember hearing tell about him. He done the same in several places. He'd get a tight foundation in, up to a few feet above ground, with windows all around, and stone steps down into it. Then, when he and his folks could, they'd put up a meetinghouse on top of it and use the basement for a vestry. Finally they'd get the steeple and the bell. By then the Elder was about ready to go off and start another foundation. You could always tell one of the Elder's churches, they used to say, because you had to go outside to get into the vestry. I—d forgot about it, but it comes back to me."

Long said, "Yes, well, that's how it happened that . . ."

Grammy Grace had followed Short and the suitcases from Old State down the stone steps and past the thick, weatherbeaten Christian door into a large, low-ceilinged room with high windows. It had a battered piano in it, a television set, two long curving sofas, several scooped-out wicker chairs, and a low table at every armrest. Still it seemed half-empty.

"Bet you this is the biggest living room in Great Country," said Short, proudly. "And the biggest kitchen, at least in any house. If you can call this a house."

He opened folding doors into a long narrow room with a long narrow table, some old-fashioned kitchen chairs of oak with caned seats, a tremendous black iron sink, red with rust, and a startlingly modern range, dishwasher, disposal, combination washer and dryer.

"The electrical equipment belongs to Jan and me, of course," said Short. "Like the tube, and everything in the living room but the old piano. The piano was left here because nobody can figure how to get it out until the walls come down. It's quite a mystery how it ever got in. The kitchen table and chairs were here, too, and we said they might as well be left. We kind of wish we could take them with us when we go, but the new kitchens aren't anywhere near big enough to take the table."

"You won't be staying here long?"

"Can't. They'll tear it down any day. And the wall. They can build three, maybe four houses on this ground."

"And the sink?" asked Grammy Grace, putting her hand on it.

Short shrugged. "Chances are that will either be buried or towed out to sea." Then as she did not move her hand he said, "You like it? Crazy, but we kind of do, too. Rust and all."

"Kerosene would take that off."

"What's kerosene?"

"Coal oil. Midway still delivers it to Old State."

"Never heard of it."

She shook her head a little, in mock despair, smiling faintly. Suddenly he reached for her elbow, chuckling with something like affection.

"Come see where you can sleep. Beds are even all made up clean. Jan always leaves them that way when we go back to work."

There were two small rooms off the living room, one on each side of the stone steps leading down from the yard, each with two small, high windows and shelves filling the inside wall beside the door. Obviously once Sunday School classrooms. The only furnishings now were a double spring and mattress in one room and three single mattresses in the other.

"Will these do?" asked Short, almost anxiously.

"Very nicely. I don't have to have legs on my bed. I'm still quite spry about getting up and down. But chances are George will have to have the single mattresses piled one on top of another or when he goes to bed he'll be cast for the duration."

"I'll fix that right now," said Short. As he worked, folding linen and slinging mattresses, he went on. "You use a lot of words that are a foreign language to me. Like kerosene and cast."

"Comes of getting out of contact with your past. George and I are part of your past, you know."

"That right? I never thought about it. Do you have names?"

"Oh, for heaven's sake. Of course we have names. George Peterson and Grace Murkle. But you aren't supposed to call us by them."

"Why not?"

"Because while we're here we're standing in for the grandparents you never saw. Call him Gramp and me Gram."

He grinned. "Call me Roddy."

"I will."

"I know some people named Peterson."

"They may be George's real grandchildren. He'd surely like to see them."

"I don't know anyone named – what did you say your last name is?"

"Murkle. I was an only child and never married. My father had no brothers. My pupils were my children."

"You were a teacher?"

"For forty-five years."

"Part of them here?"

"No, always in Midway. I was born there when it was East, and was the age to stay when it became Midway. That was really not so very long ago, Roddy."

"Seems as if it must have been, – Gram."

"It wasn't. Only about thirty-five years. But a lot can happen in thirty-five years."

Grampy George came in then with Long, whom he was calling Max, and was shown around. He felt drawn to the piano as Grammy Grace had been to the sink, and when Roddy opened it for him he tried a few of the keys.

"Needs tuning," he said.

"Needs something," said Max cheerfully. "Needs dumping, if you ask me."

"Needs tuning," repeated Grampy George.

"Pianos we have in our Rec Halls – houses aren't big enough for them – never seem to need anything. They're pounded within an inch of their lives, too."

"If they don't, they will," said Grammy Grace. "Everything goes out of whack in time. That's when it needs a little tender, loving care."

"We get a new one," grinned Max.

"Which may not be as good."

"May be better."

"How do you know, if you haven't seen what tender, loving care does for the old one?"

"Answer her that if you can, Max," said Roddy, coming out of the bedroom. "But I'll tell you right now there'll be no end to the argument until you give up. So what do you say if we take off out of here so they can unpack, or clean up, or rest, or whatever they want to do? The bathroom's at the end of the kitchen, Gramp. And there's foodstuff in the cupboards and refrigerator.''

"Okay," Max said. "Just call if you want anything. We'll be in the car."

"Haven't you got better places to go than that?" asked Grampy George.

"Plenty," Roddy assured them. "But we're on duty. We're standing guard over you as long as you're in Two State."

"Standing guard!" scoffed Grammy Grace. "Does anybody think people our ages can climb that wall or that gate and get wherever it is they don't want us to be?"

"After what happened to the Keogh and Ryan boys, just about everybody who has kids thinks you probably can fly over walls or walk right through locked doors and gates," Max said. "My wife for one. She'll never take her eyes off any of our three until you've left the state. If then. She even hates my having this assignment, and then Jan tells her we let you off The Rescue she'll think you've put a spell on me."

"They think we're witches, George,"

said Grammy Grace. "Did you ever!"

"You're strangers," said Max. "Nobody knows what a stranger can or will do. Besides, you have to admit you've been mixed up in some mighty funny business."

"Nothing funny about it," garrumphed Grampy George. "Two boys got restless. Wanted to see their grandparents. Didn't know it. Didn't know they had any. But that's what they wanted. It's human nature. And they got shown the way."

"How did they get shown the way? That's the big question."

"Ask the boys. They'll tell you."

"You don't know?"

"Yes, we know. But likely none of you would believe us. Ask the boys."

"Do you two think we're witches?" asked Grammy Grace.

"Not witches," said Max slowly. "I don't know what you are."

"I'm taking you at your word," said Roddy. "You're grandparents. But you must see that's just about as strange to us here as witches would be. We don't know what grandparents are. Max and I are beginning to find out, but nobody else – except those two boys ' has any idea. . . . Look at it this way. We at least know you need food and beds and a chance to move around, like anybody else. We know you can't climb walls or go through locked doors and gates. But this state is crowded with people who don't even know that, and after what's happened all they want is to be rid of you. Max and I are on guard a lot more to see that nobody else gets in here than to see you don't get out. Right, Max?"

Max nodded.

"That's about it. It's our job to deliver you safe to Midway. You should have agreed to go today but you wouldn't. And somehow I couldn't face keeping you in that plane with Spike glaring and growling at you while you were making up your minds. So Roddy and I've taken on quite a responsibility. Our slipping up might bring on anything, up to and including civil war.

We know that better than Midway does, because Midway thinks it has Two State under control, and we know it hasn't."

"I see," said Grammy Grace softly. "Well, I can tell you you know more about grandparents than you think you do. You know how to treat grandparents – with courtesy and forbearance and respect for the infirmities of age. It was very stubborn of Gramp and me to insist on staying and cause you so much trouble and your state so much anxiety, but you can be sure we had a reason and we hope and believe that when we go, you will all know the reason and think it was a good one and worth your trouble. In the meantime, we deeply appreciate your hospitality and your protection. Now, if, as Roddy suggested, you want to go outside for a while, we'll call you as soon as we're righted round here."

The sun was just setting when she called them back, and there was a rosy glow from the high windows lying in streams through the room where once children had been assembled for prayer before separating into classes for Sunday School. Grampy George was snoring in his room, but she had made a fruit punch with the juice from frozen raspberries, ginger ale, and grapefruit juice, and filled a frosty pitcher. She brought out a tray of crackers, too, which she had sqread with something spicy and toasted in the oven.

"Now you boys take off your coats and ties and relax for a while," she said, "while I get us some supper."

"What's this thing you've tied on?" asked Roddy. It was a pink square with little blue flowers on it, and a big bow-knot in the back.

"An apron."

"Where'd you get it? Jan never had anything like that."

"Brought it with me, of course. Just three things I couldn't be overnight without. My toothbrush, a comb, and an apron. Bet you itch to untie that bow."

He nodded.

"Hm," said Grammy Grace. "Boys always have. Well, don't you dare!"

She disappeared into the kitchen.

She could not hear them talking. It must have been the tinkle of ice and glass that roused George. After he came out there was talk enough, and louder sounds. He and Max told Roddy about Elder Walmsley, which reminded George of other people who had lived in Two State when he was a boy and this was West State. These reminiscences led to many half-incredulous questions from Roddy and Max about what life was like here then, and George was more than happy to answer them, even though he kept drowning out part of a question of part of an answer by thumping on the piano.

Max was the first to darken the kitchen door.

"Something out here smells skrip," he said.

"Is that good or bad?" asked Grammy Grace, closing the oven door.

"The best, in New language when we

lived there. No knowing how they say it now. That's where all the national slang originates, of course. Oh, the kids in Midway try to start some, they get so bored with their teachers' expressions and what they hear their parents say on vacations; but they forget all their own and most of the old stuff as soon as they get to New which is really the national mother lode for slang. I think in Midway they used to say fantastic for what I mean by *skrip*. Or maybe tops. Anyway, what is it?"

"Might be one thing, might be another. When I get it on the table, you can find out what taste matches whatever smell you're referring to."

"How soon will that be?"

"Ten minutes, if you don't stand there saying interesting things that have to be translated."

He grinned, saluted, and left. Through George's thumping and another question from Roddy she heard the creak of the outside door and felt the jar as it closed.

"I suppose he's gone out to survey the parapets," she thought, amused. "Well, I hope the attackers don't come until after we've eaten, for Jan doesn't stock what I'd call a full larder. That is, she's by no means ready to be snow-bound here for a week. Have to grant that in this weather she has no reason to expect snow."

But Max had gone for flowers and came back with a sprawling handful of roses, old-fashioned Crimson Ramblers which Elder Walmsley or his people must have set out inside the churchyard wall and which still climbed and bloomed there, though sparsely.

"Seen anything we can put these in? Paper cup or anything?"

"I think I spied an old bowl on the top shelf. See if you can reach it."

The bowl was cracked. When Max filled it with water, drops oozed out.

"Set it on a plate," said Grammy Grace. "We'll watch to see it doesn't overflow. Shouldn't be surprised if that bowl was used for chowder, back when they used to have clam suppers here. Makes me clam-hungry just to think of it."

"Clam?"

"Shellfish. We used to go to the beach and dig them at low tide when I was a child. All we could get free for the digging. Of course they were declared unsafe – because of pollution – before you can remember."

"'That's Midway for you. Their industry has polluted the whole coastline."

"Comes of trying to provide us all with more things than we need or should want. Remember that when you're a Midwayan.... All right. Tell Gramp and Roddy I'm dishing up."

"Chow!" yelled Max.

Roddy came at a gallop.

They walked up and down beside the long table, asking what was this and what was that.

This was a platter of canned chicken fricasseed and poured over what had been frozen peas. That was a basket of crusty hot cheese biscuits wrapped in a cloth. This was a dish of carrot sticks on ice, and that was chopped cabbage and apple with a few raisins, mixed with Grace's own boiled dressing. . . . Iced tea. Iced coffee. Lemon slices. . . . A big raspberry pie with crisscross crust. The left-over piecrust spread with butter, sprinkled with sugar and cinnamon, rolled, cut into squares and baked at the same time as the pie. A boiled custard with lemon sauce, because pie gave George indigestion.

"It all smells skrip," Max said.

Roddy nodded.

"Where'd you find all this stuff?"

"Well, I found what I found. Jan probably does better than I can with what comes out of packages and freezers and cans. But if you're as hungry as I am it will probably do you. GEORGE! What are you hanging back for? Supper's ready."

He came in from the living room, rolling down his sleeves.

"Nobody told me –"

Max said, "I told you, Gramp. I said CHOW."

"That mean supper? Thought maybe you was calling a dog Roddy had here and I hadn't seen. Been trying to tune that danged piano –"

"Sit down, Gram. So we can."

Roddy pushed her chair in.

She smiled at him, saying, "Thank you, Roddy."

As the men were choosing places, Max said, "You know, don't you, Roddy, Laurel would say we're crazy to eat this; maybe Jan, too?"

"Not going to stop me, I can tell you."

"Me, either. How do we get it on the plates?"

"You serve yourself," said Grammy Grace. "There's a big spoon beside each dish. We call it family style." Then, as Max reached for the platter, "But not quite yet. We always say grace before we eat. George?"

"Bless this food to our use. In the name of our Lord, Jesus Christ, we ask it."

"Now help Gramp to some chicken, Max. Likely it's a long reach for him. And have some yourself. Plenty more in the spider."

"That's grace?" asked Roddy with a twinkle. "Thought your name was Grace."

He reached with pretended slyness for her apron strings and she slapped his hand.

"It is. There are many kinds of grace."

"Chicken in the spider?" asked Max.

"Used to be the back-country word for frypan. I never knew why. Now let's go back for me to get something clarified. Why would Laurel and maybe Jan, too, say you were crazy to eat this?"

Roddy and Max exchanged glances, their mouths too full for answering. They continued to chew and swallow appreciateively. Roddy was ready first.

Over the rim of his glass of iced coffee he said, "How do we know what you've put in it?"

"What could I put in it except what was here in the kitchen?"

"Maybe something you brought in your gear."

"My suitcase, you mean?"

"Or that thing you had on your arm. Or your apron pocket. Maybe magic powders to make it all smell and taste so skrip – and tie us to your apron strings forever. Maybe pills that will put us into a deep sleep and leave you two free to go out and hypnotize Two State adults while you and all the children fly off on broomsticks. Somebody pass me that salad or whatever it is."

"Here.... You said you knew we weren't witches."

Roddy was eating again.

Max said, "I also said everybody here who hasn't seen you thinks you are. Or something like it. Including Laurel."

"So they ought to see us."

"But the best of them won't. They don't want to. Anything but. And the rest aren't going to, if we can help it."

A bell rang.

"Telephone," said Roddy. "I'll get it."

"If it's Midway or Spike," Max told him, "call me."

It was not Midway or Spike. It was a very small voice.

"Hello. Uncle Roddy? Is Daddy there?"

"Sure is, Kitten."

"Tell him to come home. Mommy doesn't want him to stay there. Auntie Jan doesn't want you to either. They don't know I'm calling. They're outside –"

"Tell him yourself. We're okay. He's right here. . . . Max! It's Kitten –"

Roddy came back to the table.

"Hi there, Kit! . . . Kit? . . . Kit, are you on the line?. . ."

Max came back to the table.

"She's gone. Chances are Laurel caught her and made her hang up. What did she say to you, Roddy?"

"Said her mother and Jan wanted us to come over there. Said they didn't know she was calling."

"Somebody must have found out. I'll ring up Laurel later – or you might to get Jan. We can try to ease their minds. But it won't do any good." Max looked from Grace to George and back again. "Just like I told you. Everybody in Two State is terrified of you. This the last of the cheesy stuff?"

"Another panful of biscuits ready to come out of the oven."

She refilled the basket, and scraped out the spider into the platter.

"You mean your wife is afraid some harm might come to your child from telephoning here?"

"While you're here, sure. You didn't even have wires to spirit those boys away."

"I never heard of anything so – so sad!"

George said, "It's plumb ridiculous. Nobody spirited those boys away. They just went. Like boys always have and always will, once in a while. Only they went farther than most."

"Yeah, and how did they get so far?"

"On their own legs, too far to find their way back," said Grace. "And they didn't want to come back. At least, Dunwoodie didn't. So they were shown a shorter way. To us."

"Doesn't made sense. How could it be shorter to Old State than back the way they had come?"

"Did it ever occur to you there might be a shorter way to Old State than you know?"

"Well, even so, who showed them?"

"The boys will tell you. They were there. We weren't."

"Even if they're telling, we're not hearing, so we're still in the dark. Didn't they tell you?"

"'Course they told us," said George impatiently. "Grace, you know I can't eat pie."

"So I made you a boiled custard. Help yourself. Here's the sauce.... Yes, they told us, and we believed them. I only hope you people will when they tell you."

"Why shouldn't we?"

"Because you seem to be highly skeptical of anything outside your own experience. You're inclined to the belief that anything you didn't see happen didn't happen. Or else was some kind of a conjuror's trick."

Both Max and Roddy had a second piece of pie, another glass of iced coffee, while George excused himself and went back to the piano.

"I aim to have that danged thing so anybody can play on it, if they want to, before I leave here," he said over his shoulder.

Finally Max pushed back his plate.

"Watch out, Rod. Her pills may be beginning to work. I feel sleepy."

"Not me," said Roddy, putting away a last bite. "I'm howling."

"You're what?" asked Grace.

"Feeling great, to you, I guess. Satisfied. What did they use to say – oh, raring to go."

"Then for heaven's sake, go," she said. "While I clean up here."

"Let's see what's on the tube," said Max, standing and stretching.

"Can I help you, Gram?" asked Roddy.

"No, thanks. I'll do better without you. I've had you underfoot long enough."

"You're just afraid of losing that apron."

He followed Max into the living room where a blast of music was overcoming George's thumping.

Grace smiled to herself, stacking plates, rinsing knives and forks. This was almost like a family, as she had once known families. It was pleasant being sole mistress of a kitchen, the only woman in the house.

But a minute later Max shouted, "Gram! Come quick! Gramp, stop that noise and come look! There's a Two State conclave starting! A panel discussion of the Problem of the Hour! And you're it!"

They were indeed.

A group of young people with

handsome faces faced each other on either side of a long table at the end of which another like them was speaking. All were dressed in what looked like peacock feathers.

"Assuming that all children are safely in bed and beyond reach of our voices, we will now proceed to the discussion of this matter which is foremost in all our minds and will be, at least until our state is rid of these two intruders. Our switchboards have been lit up all afternoon with your calls, and messages are coming in constantly. All messages have been or are being carefully recorded and we shall deal with as many communications as possible in this program, No Limit, which as you know usually runs for about an hour but in this emergency may well continue all night. We assure you that we fully understand and share your deep concern. . . ."

"What are they wearing?" asked Grace.

"What is always worn in the evening

on the tube. Artificial feathers, treated to bring out all the colors of the spectrum with high iridescence."

It was certainly a brilliant display. Blinding, was what it was.

"They men or women?" asked George.

"Both."

"How can you tell?"

"By their voices."

"That's good, George," said Grace. "We can shut our eyes."

The discussion had started and was already flowing like water over a mighty falls.

These two creatures who had by some occult means or extraordinary trickery managed for totally incomprehensible reasons of their own to spirit two boys into Old State and convince them that they had been directed there by some presumably supernatural figure, and detained them there for two weeks, working no one knew what strange influences on them (allowed to do this by the disgusting weakness of Midway and its infuriating authoritarianism), and returned them only when forced to do so by fear of the violent emotions erupting in Two State – yes, it was true that two Old Staters had flown in with the boys to Two State on The Rescue and that they were no longer on it. Certainly they were supposed to have been every minute under guard of six secret servicemen. This Two State had been promised and firmly assured of by Midway. That they had escaped might naturally be attributed to the typically poor planning of Midway, as many were doing; but it must be remembered that all secret servicemen employed by Midway were of course residents of Two State. Who else had the capacity for such duty? Five of those men had children here. All six had wives here. This had been carefully checked out. Four of those men were now themselves under heavy guard on The Rescue. The other two, it must be admitted, had disappeared with the intruders and were definitely involved in their escape.

However, it was most important that the names of these men not be revealed until all possibilities for dealing with this matter had been explored. The mood of Two State was such that any impulsive action might result in serious injustice to some of their own citizens. The servicemen now in custody of Two State police claimed that the other two had left The Rescue and driven the intruders away in a car belonging to one of them, not only apparently clearly aware of what they were doing but with the approval of the government in Midway. So far it had been impossible to communicate with any official in Midway who would state that he had authorized anyone's leaving the plane. No one here would be surprised by anything Midway might authorize. That was really immaterial. The important question was what had motivated two Two State citizens to fly in the face of public opinion in this crisis. It seemed incredible that they would do so unless under very strange influences. Those who could convince children that they had found and talked with an old man living alone above the treeline on Great Mountain and then so attach those children to themselves that those children, finally home, could think of little else but the wish to find and be with them again – such extraordinary creatures might have very different but equally effective ways of dealing with adults, even strong young men. Great care must be exercised. Yes, it was true that after the Ryan boy had told his brothers and sisters of his experiences not only he but three of them had disappeared for a time, but he and two of them had since been rounded up. They admitted to having been searching for those they called Grampy George and Grammy Grace. They had been locked in their bedroom by their father and were said to be in a rebellious condition. Police and others hoped soon to come upon the fourth Ryan child. The Dunwoodie boy, reacting less belligerently and being constantly watched and carefully restrained, refused to eat and was often in tears. This day which had been so long anticipated as one of relief and rejoicing in Two State was instead a sad one with ever heightening tension. But it could be declared unequivocally that Two State police did know where the two Old Staters and the two secret servicemen were holed up, that they were completely surrounded at a little distance, that it was impossible for any of them to make any direct personal contact with Two Staters, and that as soon as possible – conducive to the physical and psychological safety of the two servicemen – the Old Staters would be returned to The Rescue and flown immediately to Midway. The Rescue pilot had sworn that he would die before he would bring them back here, regardless of who might order it, and it was his belief that every other pilot – all, of course, Two Staters in the employ of Midway airlines – would take the same stand. In the meantime, the most fruitful discussion which could be engaged in had to do with what steps Two State could take to become completely self-sufficient, establish its independence from Midway, acquire the additional land it must have for its rapidly increasing population, and secure its absolute impregnability. The present situation was intolerable, and therefore –

"Hold on right here," said George. "Turn that thing off, one of you boys. I've heard enough. Have they all gone crazy? Sounds as if they're trying to turn this state into an armed camp. What's this fuss about the Ryan young ones? According to Chuck, they've all been let to run free as soon as they could walk, and it's worked out all right. Never saw one of Chuck's age better at looking after himself. Now all of a sudden they're locking them up? No wonder they're mad!"

"We've been telling you," Roddy said, "parents are scared to death of you, And it's catching " He glanced uneasily at the high windows.

"Poppycock!" said Grace. "Scared of an old woman they – some of them – used to go to school to and an old man with a crampy leg who only wants to be left alone to tune a piano. This carrying on will have Dunwoodie down sick. He's a bright, intelligent child and he'll get a long way if only he can have a little peace."

"Everybody thinks he's been a hell of a lot too far already," growled Max.

"Watch your language," said George. "There's a lady here. . . . Grace, how we going to get those young ones out of solitary?"

"Looks like there's just one way," Grace told him. "I mean one move that's essential. We've got to leave."

"At last you're talking sense," said Max, springing to his feet. "Come on. Grab your stuff and let's get out of here. We may be surrounded but they'll let us through when I tell them we're headed for the airport. Plenty of them will tail us there."

"Too bad," Roddy said. "I was hoping to find out what you'd put together for breakfast, Gram. But way they're talking I might never have, anyway. Let's go."

"No. Not yet," Grace said firmly. "That wouldn't do at all. If we just disappear we won't have accomplished anything by coming – just given the children a terrible day, which is the last thing anybody in Old State sent us here for. Max, you go to the telephone and call up that station and tell them to send some equipment over here. George and I've got things to say to Two State and as soon as it's on tape we'll go. Not before."

"That's impossible," said Max. "Nobody will bring television equipment in here and run it. Can't you understand? It would be more likely if you had a plague. A – lot more likely."

"Much is possible that you wont know of," snapped Grace. "Roddy, you call them. You will, won't you? Is that so much to ask? That you try?"

Roddy looked uncomfortable.

"Max is my superior officer, remember."

"Oh, I'm not stopping you," Max said, pacing the room. "I won't do it, and make a fool of myself, but if you want to, go ahead. Then they'll know you've been black-magicked, and they'll see that we all get out of the state within half an hour, hoping you and I'll be thrown into a decompression chamber as soon as we get to Midway and kept there until we have our feet on the ground. I can't deny I got us into this mess. Maybe this is the quickest way to get us out."

Roddy drew a deep breath and began dialing.

"Don't imagine for a minute they're going to make any tapes, or do anything but see that we all get out of here fast," Max warned the Old Staters. "You'd better be repacking those bags."

"The fastest way," Grace said, sitting with folded hands, "is to send the equipment right over. Soon as it's set up we can say all we have to say in half an hour, and be off."

George went back to thumping on the piano.

"Hello. Rod McTavish speaking. Connect me with Mint Waverly, please. . . . Mint? Rod McTavish. . . . Yeah. Thought my name would get me through to you. . . . I know you know where I am. We've just been tuned in on No Limit. . . . Max Schofield and the two from Old State – you know that, Mint. Don't waste my time. What's the idea? If you're trying to find out whether I know where I am and who I'm with, I do. . . . Sure Max and I have a lot of accounting to do and we'll do it later. But first it looks like we've got to get out of this gravity-pull or the whole state will be berserk. Now hang tight and listen – these two Old Staters are determined to speak to Two Staters. The minute they have, they promise to leave peacefully and immediately and we'll fly them to Midway. They've agreed, after hearing some of the broadcast, to settle for a taped interview for the tube. So what we want is for you to send the equipment to my house as fast as possible and make the tape, to get us all off the hook. . . . They don't have to come in, dope. They can work through my windows on the north side."

"Never thought of that," muttered Max, brightening.

"Of course you don't: That's moonshot. Just send the stuff and make the tape. Minute it's made we're heading for the airport at a hundred an hour if the streets are cleared. . . . glorific. The sooner the better."

Roddy turned from the telephone and said, "They're coming."

"Very good," said Grace, rising. "Now we'll pack. Come, George."

"I ain't unpacked," said George. "I've almost got this danged piano so you can play on it while I sing about Davy Crockett to the young ones. It always tickles Chuck and Dun when I sing to 'em about Davy Crockett."

"I take it it's all right to say 'danged' to a lady," grinned Roddy.

"Just barely acceptable," said Grace, flouncing off.

"So what's the matter with 'hell'?" asked Max.

"You have to change at least one letter," said George, between thumps.

"Like there'd be no objection to saying anybody had gone a helium of a lot too far?" asked Roddy. "That changes three letters!"

"Still indicates a shockingly poor vocabulary," called Grace from what was to have been her bedroom. "On the part of both of you."

"Goes to show we didn't stay in school long enough," said George. "They say schooling makes all the difference."

"It's not how long you stay, at all," said Grace, returning. "It's how much you get out of it while you're there. Now I'll see what I can do about those dishes before –"

The telephone rang. Max picked

it up.

"Right. . . . I'll be there." He replaced the receiver. "The truck from TTS is on the way. I'll open the gate when it pulls up."

He went outside. Roddy offered again to help with the dishes and this time was not refused.

"I don't want Jan to come home to a dirty kitchen," said Grace. "I don't believe a woman ever lived who didn't resent that."

George continued to thump.

There was the roar of motors. The gate creaked open and clanged shut. Max came in and threw up the north windows, went out again.

"Want to take out some biscuits to the crew?" Grace asked. "Pie? Pudding?"

"Nobody would dare eat them, cheers, cheers," said Roddy. "I only hope they'll keep till Jan and I get back."

He took the bowl of roses into the living room and put it on a coffee table. Then he lowered shades evenly along the south wall, and emptied ashtrays. If by any chance this film was ever shown, he and Jan would want to feel proud of their pad. Not many would even think of it, he supposed, but they would. They liked this hole in the ground.

"All set," shouted Max triumphantly through an open window. "Rolling as soon as you say the word, Gram!"

"Now you can untie my apron, Roddy."

"Now I don't want to. On you it looks good. Keep it on."

She went in and paused by the bowl of roses. George was still on the piano bench but no longer thumping.

She said quietly, "Turn around, George. The children will like your face better than your back. . . . Shall we begin, Max?"

"Lift off! Roll it, astros –"

"Good evening, Two State. I hope some of you will remember me as one of your teachers in Midway. In your time there I taught English in Dalton Junior High. I am Miss Murkle. Grace

Murkle. Others of you may remember George Peterson, who is here with me visiting your state. He was a cabinetmaker in what was the Kenworth area of Midway and those of you who lived in that area may have used kitchen cupboards, counters, built-in appliances and other expert carpentry which was his work, and may have watched him doing it. More importantly, several of you must be his own grandchildren. But of course you all left Midway for New State quite a while before we left it for Old State, and so much has happened in your lives since then that you may have forgotten. Please try now to remember.

"Try to remember because, if you can, it will be easier for you to believe what we are going to tell you – first, that we are the same people, only older, that we were when we lived in Midway with you, just as you are the same people you were when you were Midway residents, only older. Neither moving nor time dehumanizes anyone, unless he allows himself to be dehumanized; and I assure you we haven't.

"We are your friends. We consider ourselves both your grandparents and the representatives of all your grandparents in Old State. No one ever has more loyal, understanding, and indulgent friends than his grandparents. To fear us is unreasonable, and such fear comes only of lack of knowing us. We came hoping to make ourselves better known to you, and to get to know you. We now see that the latter is impossible at present, except for what we have been able to learn of you from Roddy McTavish and Max Schofield who have most graciously entertained us for several hours. Thus we are about to leave your state, according to your wish, but before we go we want to try through this medium to make ourselves better known to you.

"Now, Mrs. Keogh, will you wake Dunwoodie if he has gone to sleep and bring him to where he can see and hear us? And, Mrs. Ryan, will you let Chuck come to the television? If we may speak to others of the children of Two State – even all of them – at the same time, it will be a pleasure to us and, I believe, to them, and may help to solve many of their and your problems which have so unnecessarily and unfortunately been created, during recent weeks, by misapprehension.

"Dunwoodie and Chuck just returned today from a visit to Old State. It was a visit totally unexpected by them and by us. For us a happy surprise and for them, I think, an enriching experience. We all loved them on sight, and they learned to love us. For hundreds of years it has always been like this with grandparents and their grandchildren whenever they had a chance to be for a while undisturbed in a private world of their own. The very young and the very old have more in common than any other two age segments of society. They need each other, not all the time, but every now and then. They have a special hunger for each other, though children who have not known grandparents cannot know what it is they hunger for. Dunwoodie and Chuck now know, and in that and one other way – but only those two ways – are changed from what they were when they left you and are different from those who did not go with them. Try to understand and accept this, parents and children both. They have been 'away to school.' Now they have come home, bringing exciting new knowledge. Don't ignore it. Don't repress it. We found both to be absoluely truthful and each, in his own way, gifted in communication. Listen to them, and learn from them. This, I assure you, is an absolute essential to the future of Two State and of Great Country. Later I will try to tell you why we are convinced of this.

"But now I want to talk directly to Chuck and Dunwoodie, though all you other children are more than welcome to listen just as you would in school if your teacher was talking especially to one or two of your classmates. . . . We miss you tonight, boys, and everyone in Old State where you have been visiting misses you, too. But we had a lovely visit together, and the happier a visit is the sooner it seems to come to an end. You have had a long, busy day – said many good-byes, had a long ride in a plane, and got home again where probably everything that used to be so familiar seems a little bit strange. But when you wake up tomorrow morning it will all seem natural to you again and you will have as many hellos to say as you said good-byes today. Life is like that.

"As I said, Grampy George and I miss you, but as you can see we're not giving in to it. We know we are lucky to have had you with us. Now you need your own families and playmates, and other, older people need us. At least, we think they do. We have been visiting in Mr. Rod McTavish's house which we like very much. Grampy George likes it especially because it is part of an old church and he has heard of the old Elder who built it a long time ago. Imagine that! Maybe you can come to see it someday. Ask your parents to bring you quite soon, because there is nothing else like it in your whole state and we hear that it is scheduled to be torn down. If you have seen it, you will never forget it, and it is important that it shouldn't be forgotten because it is part of the history of your country. It has a kitchen where I cooked supper tonight for Mr. McTavish and Kit Schofield's daddy and us. We had that pudding you like to share with Grampy George, Chuck, and it was all eaten up; but you both liked my cheese biscuits and quite a few of them were left. If you know Jan McTavish and live near enough, maybe she would give you each one, or even two, if you ask her. They are small enough, remember, to carry in your pockets.

"There is a piano here too. It was quite out of tune but Grampy George has been working on it and thinks it is improved. So I'm going to play it now for him to sing you that song you like about Davy Crockett. At the end of the third verse he will point up toward the ceiling (that is to remind you of the Man on the Mountain who told you the way to go to get to Old State) and I will turn round on the piano bench and smile at you (that will be saying goodnight), and then we want you to go to your beds and get into them. Ask your mothers to leave the doors open, if there are doors between, for Grampy George will go right on singing through the other verses. When he finishes, we hope you will be sound asleep – Dunwoodie and Chuck and all you children – and have good dreams and wake up rested and eager to find out what is going to happen tomorrow. For none of us ever knows just what is going to happen until it happens. And we want to be ready. . . ."

Grammy Grace took off her apron, folded it neatly, and put it on the arm of the sofa. She took a red rose from the bowl and pinned it among the little curls on he top of her head. Then she sat down on the piano bench, Grampy George having slid up to one end of it. He was looking toward the cameras and her back was to them. But before she began to play she turned and said:

"Now this isn't saying goodnight, of course. That will be the next time I turn around. But the way we're sitting reminds me of a double chair that my mother and father had in our best room when I was a little girl. There was a seat facing one way and another seat facing the opposite way, and they were attached and all upholstered in green velvet, so that two people sitting there could look at each other. It was called a courting chair. I just had to tell you about it because probably you have never seen one. I never have since, and that was a long time ago."

"I don't calculate," said Grampy George, "you young ones know what the word 'courting' means and Grammy Grace must think that's just as well or she'd explain it to you. As you can see, she's a great one for explaining things. . . . And after all the time she's took up she'd better not send you to bed before I even start. I may not be much at singing but I'm better at that than I am at talking so you just set still there and keep quiet if you want to hear about Davy Crockett."

Grammy Grace played a few chords. Grampy George cleared his throat and began in a reedy but deep bass:

Davy, Davy Crockett, king of the wild frontier.
Off through the woods he's a-marchin' along
Makin' up yarns an' a-singin' a song
Itchin' fer fightin' an' rightin' a wrong
He's ringy as a b'ar an' twice as strong.
Davy, Davy Crockett, the buckskin buccaneer! . . .

Fought single-handed through the Injun War

Til the Creeks was whipped an' peace
was in store,
An' while he was handlin' this risky
chore,
Made hisself a legend for evermore.
Davy, Davy Crockett, king of the
wild frontier!

He give his word an' he give his hand
That his Injun friends could keep
their land,
An' the rest of his life he took the
stand
That justice was due every redskin
band.
Davy, Davy Crockett, holdin' his
promise dear.

At the end of the third verse Grammy Grace poked him with her elbow and he glared at her and then grinned and pointed toward the ceiling. She turned smiling – actually she was laughing – and said softly in a kind of singing, "Good-night, dear children," before turning again to the piano. The

rose had slipped from the top of her head and now clung trembling to the back. Grampy George sang on.

He went off to Congress an' served a spell,
Fixin' up the Gover'ment an' laws as well,
Took over the Capitol so we heered tell
An' patched up the crack in he Liberty Bell.
Davy, Davy Crockett, seein' his duty clear!. . .

His land is biggest an' his land is best,
From grassy plains to the mountain crest,
He's ahead of us all meetin' the test
Followin' his legend into the west.
Davy, Davy Crockett, the man who don't know fear!

When the song was ended Grace did not get up again, just swung around on the bench. The rose had fallen off.

George, grunting faintly, picked it up and tossed it into her lap. She sat thinking, spreading its petals gently with one forefinger. He sat bent a little forward, a hand spread on each knee, rubbing his knees slowly and staring at what movement he could see beyond the open windows.

Finally she said, "Now that the children have all gone to sleep – we hope! – I want to speak to you who are their parents and friends, to give you, before we go, the message their, and your, friends in Old State sent you by us. Remember I said earlier it is essential that you listen to what Chuck and Dunwoodie have to tell you about the time they have been away, and believe them. Now I want to tell you why it is essential.

"First, because they are bright, well-balanced, truthful boys so what they tell you will be the truth and all of us in Great Country – everywhere in the world – need all the knowledge of truth we can get. We must know what is true if we are to survive as a race and we cannot discover a great part of it from our personal experiences under the restricions with which we now live, so we must seize every possible opportunity to learn from others what they have learned.

"Second, because they are the only people who have really overcome one of the barriers which have grown up or been thrown up between the people of Great Country. They really broke through one, small as they are, and though the opening is proportionately small it is enormously important and we, for our part, intend to do all we can to hold it open. They can tell you much that we cannot, because they know your language as we don't. Now they also know our language, our way of life, our feeling toward them, and their feeling toward us, and will explain it to you if you will let them. They need to explain it to you, and then to have you share it with them insofar as you possibly can.

"We hoped that our coming would

make this easier for them and for you. We hope now that seeing and hearing from us in this way will help you to understand that the people of Old State are just human beings who have grown old as our grandparents and parents grew old and as you will grow old in time. We think one reason why you fear us and want to isolate and forget us is because you find the thought of your own eventual aging unacceptable and intolerable; and we regret this attitude of yours deeply both for our own sakes and for yours. Because the truth is that becoming old is nothing to be dreaded; though it brings its own problems it solves or eases others, and has many advantages; if you did not have this wrong impression we could be very useful to you and your children, as our grandparents were to us. And, for our part, what we most feel the lack of is the opportunity to know, enjoy, and be useful to the young.

"I assume many – perhaps all – of you assume that the world has now changed so much that what the old know and can do is no longer of any interest to you. If so, I can only say that you are mistaken. The world could not change that much while human beings still populate it. It is precisely because you do not know what we know and can do that you do not realize we have knowledge and skills you don't have and therefore don't understand how much you need them or what it is you need – any more than children who have never known their grandparents understand their own grandparent-hunger.

"Some of you have been talking on your No Limit program tonight about plans to become completely self-sufficient, establish your independence from Midway, and so on. One of the things we of Old State know is that no age group, no individual, is ever completely self-sufficient, and it is not total independence from Midway that you want and need but to be represented there to have Midway and the other states represented here, and thus to begin the process of the reintegration of Great Country which is essential to the future of us all. You must not continue to blind yourselves to the fact that Midway is not only the government, but is your parents, the people you grew up with and who did a good deal to make you what you are, and is the place which you will soon go to and take over and in which you will be laden like Atlas with unrewarding responsibilities, and see your children leave you forever, and stay to the day you are sent to confinement until death in Old State, unless you use your youthful strength and develop the drive and ability to start bringing an end to this horrible separateness instead of adding to it.

"In a very few minutes now we are leaving to fly on to Midway. There we are to try to represent Old State to our sons and daughters. (My pupils were the only sons and daughters I have ever had.) On the basis of what we have seen of and learned from two of your children and Max Schofield and Roddy

McTavish we shall also do our best to speak for you. We hope that, putting together what you have seen and heard of us now with what Chuck and Dunwoodie will tell you, you will no longer harbor the notion that we are 'extraordinary creatures' in any way, or deal in the occult, or engage in trickery, or would ever intentionally do anything inimical to your best interests. We are your fellow-citizens. We came here as your friends and we leave here as your friends. We are your grandparents, we love you, and we hope you will develop the capacity to love us. It is not enough to love only your children and one another, for your children will leave you – permanently, unless we quickly cooperate on steps to prevent it – and your contemporaries will be found wanting the more you concentrate on them and expect of them.

"Now I have just one more thing to say.

"It is the most important thing, and it

will be difficult for you to believe. Please trust me, and try.

"Dunwoodie and Chuck have apparently told you that the day they left here they met and talked with a Man on Great Mountain. If you encourage them, they will tell you more about this experience. They told us, and we believed them, though none of us has ever seen this Man.

"We believed them because it is as incredible to us as to you that they found their own way over the mountain from Two State to Old State. They must have had help. They must have been guided.

"We believed them because the first thing they did when they crossed the boundary was to put up a sign they said He had told them to put up. Dunwoodie printed it and could not spell the long word quite right. Their sign reads 'Man on Montin.'... We believed them because we found them to be truthful, reliable boys of whom you can all be very proud. It is conceivable that Dunwoodie could have imagined such an experience, but Chuck never would, and he corroborated and contributed to every detail of Dunwoodie's account.

"And we believe them because when we were children we were told that there was a Man on Great Mountain and that a few highly favored people had found Him there. One of these was the builder of the church in the basement of which we are now sitting, old Elder Walmsley. He always told the people who gathered to hear him in one after another of the many churches he built that when he was young, hardly more than a boy, he had climbed the mountain and met there One who talked long with him, filling him with such happiness as he had never known before, and then told him to go back down the mountain and build churches – as many churches in as many places as he could – and teach the people to love one another, to trust their Creator, and to work ceaselessly for the glory of God.

"We believed Elder Walmsley then. We believe him now. And just so we believe these little boys. It has the ring of absolute truth, to us. If you cannot believe it or at best are highly skeptical of it, that surely is because you have had so little, if any, contact with the teachings of Elder Walmsley and others like him. It has, of course, been illegal to continue these teachings in any public place in Great Country since the last division of the states and the population. Few in Midway now recall them, I suppose. You and the citizens of New State probably have never heard of them. But this has not altered the status and position of the Man on the Mountain. And now two of your children have met Him, and can tell you about Him. Will you listen to them, and think of what the wisdom of such a Man would do for us, at whatever age, if we knew where and how to reach it?

"We who live in Old State are now too old to search Great Mountain for Him. Many of us did go into the foothills looking for Him when we were young, but we did not have the need of reaching

Him that you have because He spoke to us through His Elders. You do not have such Elders. We continue to live as well as we can by their teachings. You have not had the benefit of such teachings. If you are ever to know Him, at least one of you must find Him, and bear witness with the boys For one to find Him, almost certainly many must search.

"If you cannot believe that He is there, can't you believe that He may be there? For if by any chance He is, you surely want to know it beyond the shadow of a doubt. Because if ever you do know it, it will change your life and your country in wondrous ways, not only in your own minds – as it does in ours – but, because you are young and strong, in the minds of all those you reach and influence. It will change Two State in the ways it should be changed. It will take you into Midway and change Midway. You will carry it to New State – or New State will come to you for it – and it will change New State. And then some of you will bring to us the best, the most joyous news we could possibly hear – that Great Country is again one nation under God.

"Someone has said on your No Limit that you must have more territory for your rapidly growing population. Your grandparents lovingly urge you, humbly beg you, to begin by moving into the foothills instead of avoiding them, and sending exploring parties – perhaps a dozen each Sunday – toward the treeline. It is no easy climb, we know. None of us ever got that high. But two of your children did. And one day, if you try hard enough before it is too late, some of you will.

"And now, goodnight, dear children. You will never see or hear from us – any of us – again unless you wish to. You have our message. We leave the future in your hands, and in God's."

"CUT," said a voice outside the window.

Grace and George put on their coats. Grace tied a scarf over her head and hung her purse over her arm, still holding the rambler rose from the Elder's wall. George was twisting a felt hat in his hand. Max and Roddy brought out the bags and stood listening. The gate had creaked but did not clang. The roar of motors diminished into the distance.

"All clear," said Max. "Let's go."

As they rode through the deserted, dimlit streets among all the like little houses with drawn shades, Grace said suddenly, "You don't think they'll ever listen to us, do you? Maybe you don't think they even made the tape."

"It would have been easy enough not to," said Roddy.

"They taped it," growled Max.

"But you don't think they'll ever listen to it?"

"If they taped it, somebody will listen to it," said Roddy. "Out of curiosity if nothing else.

"That's what I think," said Grace happily. "And if they made it, and a few are curious enough to watch and listen to it, a lot of others will be curious enough to demand to see it too. One thing about Two Staters, – they certainly don't suffer in silence. . . . Oh, George, can you believe it? We've been to Two State and we're headed for Midway!

IV The Guys and the Dolls

There were four major airports in Midway, and by this hour their cocktail pavilions overlooking the runways were always filling up fast with Midwayans en route from the theater or late dinner to wee-hour supper atop a high-rise hotel and finally the intimate gatherings of only twenty or thirty lounging before huge windows of apartment houses to celebrate the end of another night and greet the more or less cheering dawn of another day. But tonight every pavilion at Running Brook Port – The Ginseng Tree, The Pink Champagne Grotto, The Muddy Java, The Rub-a-Drum, The Mad Dervish, The Song We Never Sang, and The Devil in Us All – was already so full that there was not even standing room inside. Waiters had given up trying to get through with trays to the tables. Motionless, silent, they sat on or stood around the bars, pressed against their gleaming surfaces and one another like miniature dark fish professionally tinned.

"Would you believe the word really got by Beaver somehow?" Sparrow Freedland asked. "Wooly said he absolutely swore the whole staff to total silence, practically on pain of reviving the death penalty. And there they all are, working away at something or nothing, locked up the way juries used to be. Wooly practically said he'd break my neck if I said one word to anybody but you."

"Same with Boulder when he called me," nodded Slipper Lee, spinning her glass between her palms.

Sparrow and Slipper had glasses because they had come in at nine o'clock to the table reserved for them and the two men they were ignoring, but it was now eleven and they had not been able to get the glasses refilled for an hour.

"You don't think it's true somebody is managing to wire-tap?"

"They'd better not, is all I can say. No, it's rumor. It wouldn't take more than a rumor. After all, when has there been even a rumor of anything as – well, as unlikely as this? Put it this way, if you had heard such a rumor, and hadn't been sent, wouldn't you have tried to get in here?"

Sparrow nodded.

"I know. I was wildly excited when we started. Now I'm just exhausted. And hot. And my head's absolutely splitting."

"Take another Be-Be. Take two. I just did."

"So did I. No good. . . . Maybe it isn't going to happen. Maybe nothing changed."

"Boulder said Beaver had absolute assurance it was going to."

Sparrow wrinkled her forehead. She had no eyebrows to raise.

She spread her hands and said, "Oh, well, then. . . ."

Suddenly a man in uniform was silhouetted at the window beside them.

The window became a door and opened. He beckoned. The men at the table rose quickly, put a blue and a rose-colored fur over the women's bare shoulders, the four stepped out into the floodlit landing area, and the door closed and locked behind them.

"The Rescue has just touched down," said the uniformed one. "It will be right in. Here it comes."

"Here? Everyone in the pavilions can see it," said Slipper.

"Doesn't matter, apparently," Sparrow murmured.

"No. The Governor's car will meet the ramp," said the uniformed one. "Just whisk them into it. We have heavy escort direct to the Mansion."

The Rescue glided to a stop. The ramp was lowered. The flagged car moved forward.

Two secret servicemen came down first, looking very grim, followed by Grace almost at a run, Roddy hurrying to keep up with her, and George proceeding more slowly and stiffly, glad of the railing on one side and Max's arm on the other.

"Oh, Miss Murkle!" cried Sparrow. "What a pleasure to welcome you to Midway! Do come right over – "

"And Mr. Peterson!" cried Slipper. "Governor Wireman sends you his most cordial greetings and is eagerly awaiting your arrival at the Mansion. He deeply regrets he could not meet the plane, but he has sent his car – "

"I am Sparrow Freedland – Mrs. Wool Freedland, you know. Or maybe you don't know. But Wool is Governor Wireman's executive assistant, and you'll be meeting him soon. And this is Slipper Lee – wife of our Lieutenant Governor, Boulder Lee. Now let me help you – "

"Oh, you'll have to wait a minute," said Grace. "George can't be hurried after he's been sitting down for a while. Besides, what about Max and Roddy?"

"Max?" asked Sparrow, doubtfully, halted in midair.

"Roddy!" said Slipper.

"You don't stay with us?" Grace asked them.

Max shook his head. "Not invited. You're being taken over by The Establishment, while we come up before the Review Board."

"To find out if we're fired," grinned Roddy. "Or Spike is. Or nobody is."

"Look here," said George, shaking hands with them. "If you're ever fired, you fly over to Old State. There'll always be a job for you there, and we'll treat you right."

"It would be only part-payment on what we owe you," said Grace. She stood on tiptoe and tugged at Max's coat until she got him down where she could kiss his cheek. He looked embarrassed but pleased. "Besides, we'd like it," she said to Roddy. "Bring Jan." When she kissed him he hugged her. Slipper and Sparrow and the two ignored men and the uniformed one stared. "We'd better go along," said Grace. "Before I start to cry."

She got quickly into the limousine,

followed by Sparrow and Slipper. The Ignored helped George in beside the women and swung into the jump seats in front of them. The door closed, the uniformed one sprang in beside the driver, the car moved and was surrounded by screaming motorcycles. Slipper touched a button and there was silence inside. Grace broke it.

"You seem to know us," she said. "Tell us again who you are, now that we can pay attention."

Slipper and Sparrow repeated the names and offices they had given before, but in more subdued, less artificially enthusiastic voices.

"Wool. Boulder. Sparrow. Slipper – I wonder if you weren't actually named Lady's Slipper?"

Slipper gasped. "How on earth did you know that?"

"Were you really?" cried Sparrow.

"So they say. But from the minute I got to New State until now nobody ever dared –"

Sparrow tittered.

"Have you ever seen a lady's-slipper?" Grace asked her.

"Not if it had a high heel. I've seen pictures of them on some library bulletin board. Deformed – "

"Pity," said Grace. "It's a lovely wildflower and grows only in forests. We still have them in Old State. I suppose you've never seen a sparrow either. Or a boulder. Or wool. Your parents were afraid you wouldn't. I well remember when your generation was being given names like that. In the hope that it would somehow keep alive good things that were disappearing – the beauty of wildflowers, the freedom of wild birds, the solidity of boulders, the gentle strength of wool. . . . Who are these gentlemen in front of us? Not your husbands, I take it."

"Heavens, no," said Slipper. "No idea who they are, really."

George put a hand on the shoulder of one of them.

"My name's Peterson," he said. "George Peterson."

The man half-turned, said, "How do you do, sir," and turned back.

"They're not supposed to say who they are," said Sparrow. "Nobody is supposed to know."

"Special secret servicemen, maybe?"

"Maybe." Sparrow shrugged.

Slipper said, "An escort is always assigned to the wife of an official if she is sent out by the administration without her husband."

"There is danger in Midway for women on official business?"

"Perhaps. We only know escorts always come for us and stay with us until we are back in our apartments."

"Don't you ask?"

"There is no one to ask. For whom we'd be likely to get an answer."

"Not even your husbands?"

Sparrow and Slipper looked at each other.

"I can't remember whether I did, at first. Did you?"

"If I did, he didn't tell me. It's just something we take for granted. They're always there and always very polite. But they don't say anything to you, and you don't to them."

"Don't hardly sound human," said George.

"Well, it certainly sounds dull," said Grace.

"It's routine," said Sparrow, shrugging again. "Like everything else."

Grace thought about that, looking out at the bright tunnel through which they were riding at high speed between massed glass and chrome buildings so tall that she could see only a narrow streak of dark sky far ahead.

Then she gave herself a small shake and turned back to her companion, smiling.

"But this isn't exactly routine, is it? Meeting The Rescue and taking two Old Staters to the – the Mansion – whatever that is? I can tell you it is far from routine to us!"

"Oh, I don't know what this is," said Sparrow. "I really haven't the slightest idea. We were told to be at Running Brook tonight, so we were. And we were told to bring two plane passengers (who would be pointed out to us) to the Mansion. Which we are doing."

"It's a little peculiar, that's all," said Slipper. She added, "The Mansion is the Capitol. It looks like the other buildings, but it is all offices and meeting rooms, except for the penthouse where the Governor and his wife live."

"And here it is," said Sparrow, drawing her rosy fur a little closer and smoothing the fingers of her pale pink gloves.

"Funny cars they've got here," said George. "Cut down from ninety miles an hour to a dead stop and you don't even lurch."

"Slipper should have your fur," Grace told Sparrow. "Lady's-slippers are pink. And you should have brown. Sparrows are brown. Speckled brown."

"I never saw brown fur," Sparrow said. "Ours are all pastel. And Slipper always chooses blue. I suppose to make her eyes look blue. But they're not. They're gray."

"You must be getting hungry, darling," said Slipper sweetly.

"Principally thirsty," said Sparrow. "I only hope Beaver has an absolute vat of those Whizzers of his."

They were stepping out of the car. A great pane of glass moved beside them, making an opening through which they passed, and moved back. A curtain fell, and George and three women – one old, two middle-aged – were alone in a great space enclosed in purple velvet curtains and occupied by what appeared to Grace in that first instant to be statues cut from marble. But then the statues came to life and were living figures – men in identical jacket and trousers of a white material resembling taffeta, crisp, with a sheen, and rustling as they walked. And there were shouts and outcries which struck the purple velvet, bounced up to the iridescent ceiling and fell back to the iridescent floor, producing a series of echoes of which the first was soft and the succeeding two sharp, staccato.

"Oh, Wooly!" ... "Well, I see you made it, Peeps!" ... "Hello, Boul!" ... "So you're back, my pet. And this must be – " ... "Mm – hm, – these are our visitors from Old State, – Miss Murkle, this is my husband." ... "Mr. Peterson, do meet Lieutenant-Governor Lee – " ... "And this is Carpenter Denham – Carpie's chargé d'affaires for your state – Ski West, Moss Ricker, Saint McGonagle, and – oh, you'll find out who they all are and what they do, I expect." ... "Ski, are there plenty of Whizzers upstairs?" ... "Who made them?" ... "Cock, I think." ... "Oh, marvelous! Did you hear? Ski thinks Cock." ... "We're absolutely exhausted, darling." ... "Who isn't?" ... "Beaver is surprised you're so late." ... "Somebody surprised beaver?" ... "Well, new combinations." ... "What are we waiting for now? ... "Programming,

programming. Two minutes in the lobby." . . . "Fifty-eight, fifty nine – " . . . "Here's the elevator!"

The elevator was completely iridescent and in the shape of a mammoth oyster. You could imagine you were riding inside an oyster shell. At least, you could try. But the numbers chasing each other around it, like purple insects playing a game in ovals, were distracting. 1 — 2 — 3 —— 7 — 10 — 12 — 22 — 37 — 41 — 53 — 65.

The shell lay still, split silently, and spewed out the two women in pastel, Grace in her decent black coat and silver lace scarf, George swaying a little, blinking, soft hat in hand, and a dozen or fifteen middle-aged men in white taffeta or reasonable facsimile.

If there was anyone or anything else except one big man in the place they had reached, nobody noticed it. The big man, in a white suit like the other men's but dripping purple cords with gold tassels, obscured all else. He stood in a blinding light and held out both big hands, his right to George and his left to Grace.

"Miss Murkle, I'm sure. And Mr. Peterson. Welcome to Midway. I am Governor Wireman, and happy indeed that you have arrived safely from Two State where, as I had feared, you were not accorded the hospitality you had requested and which I did all in my power, from this distance, to assure you. Here you may be certain you will receive every consideration. Undoubtedly, after such a trying experience, you are exhausted, so I shall myself show you to your rooms at once." Still holding Grace's and George's hands, he extended his bright, wooden smile to the rest of the group and said, "You gals and guys go on in and relax. You've earned it. Slipper and Sparrow, you will hear from my office tomorrow. I may be back later tonight and I may not. I still have a number of papers – but whether I come back or not, enjoy yourselves as long as you like. Everything is on the Mansion, of course.

Now come along, Miss Murkle, Mr. Peterson."

He touched a button, a curtain drew back, a wall rose, a floor rolled, another curtain was drawn, another wall raised, and the three stood, side by side, and hand in hand in just such a foyer as had been the entrance to Grace's little apartment when she lived and taught in Midway. The same papered walls, the little old mirror with gilded frame and eagles on the cornices hanging above the slender-legged mahogany console table which, narrow as it was, was still wide enough to obstruct passage and get in the way of the closet door when opened for the hanging up or taking down of outside wraps. . . .

"Let me have your things and I'll hang them up," said the Governor. "I'm sorry Sylvia isn't here to greet you but she isn't strong and has to go to bed very early. She told me to tell you she could hardly wait to see you at breakfast. Now come this way, please."

The followed him through a small

living room with a beige wall-to-wall carpet, an upholstered sofa with coffee table on which there were magazines; a few chushioned rocking chairs; windows along one wall with plants on the sills; a counter beyond which there were kitchen appliances; doors opening off the other two walls.

"Your rooms are rather cramped in size," said the Governor. "And I shall have to ask you to share your bath with me, Mr. Peterson, as Sylvia must share yours, Miss Murkle. We have only the two here. There are much more spacious quarters in another section but I felt that you might prefer these, at least for tonight. Tomorrow, if you like, Sylvia will show you the others. As I say, we are rather cramped here, but it is all the space that was available and we hadn't expected to have guests. Actually, you have the two bedrooms. Sylvia is sleeping in her sewing room and I shall use my study. We happen to have the extra bath because when we moved to the Mansion Sylvia had a nurse staying with her for a while."

"Too bad to put you out so," said George. "We'd have been all right in a hotel."

"Put us out?" repeated the Governor.

"He means inconvenience you," said Grace. "But let's not take any more time tonight for hospitable gesturings or polite responses. And let's not get hung up on vocabulary and definitions. I never felt so much like Alice in Wonderland in my life. I don't know about George but I, for one, shall not be able to sleep a wink until I get my feet planted on something solid. Now are you exhausted, Governor? Do you have to go to bed? Because if you don't I wish you'd just go out there for a few minutes while I wash my face and hands and get into something – oh, what has become of our suitcases?"

"They have been delivered," said the Governor, "No doubt they have been unpacked." He opened a drawer. "Aren't these your things?"

"My soul and body, so they are," said Grace. "Well, then, you men get out of here. I'll be out in ten minutes at the most. And if you're still up, Governor, and can answer me some questions, I'll be very grateful. If you feel as if you'd better go to bed, George, I'll tell you tomorrow what he said."

But when Grace reappeared George, in felt slippers and with shirt collar loosened and sleeves rolled up, was sitting at the kitchen counter smoking his pipe and the Governor, also bare-armed and wearing a canvas apron, was flipping eggs into a pan at the gas burner.

"There's toast under that cloth," said the Governor, "and that's Sylvia's rose-geranium jelly in the jar. What would you rather have to drink? Hot milk? Tea?"

"Tea for me," said George.

"Tea would be lovely," said Grace.

"Thought so," said the Governor happily. "It's already steeping."

"Steeping?" cried Grace incredulously. "You steep it?"

"Only way tea tastes like tea," said the Governor.

They huddled together at the counter over their steaming plates and cups, the buttered toast, the quivering, heavenly jelly.

"Now, Your Excellency," said Grace, a few minutes later, "I am replete. I can't stand it another minute. Here come the questions."

"Shoot," said His Excellency, chewing fast and swallowing.

"Is your name Beaver? Your people were calling somebody Beaver."

"They like to, I hear, and I don't object. Yes, that's my name."

"So you're Beaver Wireman."

"Yes."

"You went to school with me."

"I did?"

"Nursery school. The Sunlight School in Shentham."

"I don't remember, but I've been told I went there. I lived in Shentham then."

"With your grandparents. It's beginning to come back to me. Your parents never returned from moon exploration."

"My mother was the first woman to go up there."

"She must have been a remarkable person."

"I suppose she was considered so when she went. But by the time my memory begins Great Country had decided there was nothing there worth going up for, so those who remembered her at all had written her off as foolhardy. Everyone realized the first duty of young parents was to stay with their babies, and everyone was concentrating on the redistribution of population which would make this, among other things, mandatory."

'I know. After the change, when you were sent to Two State, who did you live with?"

"Aunts. I had three. They passed me around."

"You never saw your grandparents

again, of course."

"Oh, no. They were quite old. They must have gone to Old State soon after I left for Two State with the aunts. I used to dream about them a lot. I remember very little about them now."

"Consciously, you mean. It is amazing what we hold in our unconscious. Or so I was taught in college. Now, Beaver, tell me about – where we are right now; these rooms; these furnishings; this steeped tea. Nothing I've seen in Midway since The Rescue landed here had led me to expect anything like this in the Governor's penthouse at the top of the Capitol. It is all very reminiscent of the little apartment I lived in with two other teachers the last years before I was shipped out. We thought our building was the last and we were told it would soon be razed."

"It must have been. The oldest building in the state now is ten years old. . . . You sure you aren't too tired for talk? Wouldn't rather put it off until tomorrow?"

"No. I've only begun to get some answers. Besides, it must be tomorrow now."

"It's never tomorrow, I've learned," said the Governor. "And never yesterday again. Well, then, let's find more comfortable seats."

"I don't know whether I'm asleep or awake," said George. "And ain't for some time. But I know I'm of no mind to leave present company. So if I can just stretch out my legs on your couch there – "

"Go ahead," said the Governor. "I like a rocker myself. How about you, Miss Murkle?"

"A rocker's fine," said Grace. "But nobody's called me Miss Murkle for so long – until I got here – that I'm out of the habit. Why don't you call us Gram and Gramp like the young fellows in Two State did?"

"They called you Gram and Gramp? In Two State?"

"Never mind about them now. This is

Midway. I think. And while we're likely not old enough to be your grandparents we're probably near the age yours were the last time you saw them. Now. This apartment?"

The Governor said his decision to bring them here instead of assigning them quarters elsewhere had been made initially for security reasons. He had considered it essential that his discussions with them be completely private, and this apartment was the most private place in Midway. So private, in fact, that only eight people (beside himself and Sylvia) knew it existed. Six of these were the men who composed his personal, elite guard, one of whom was a doctor, one a male nurse, and two lawyers; the other two were women who attended Sylvia, a nurse and a secretary, both of whom enjoyed "playing house"; these were sworn solute secrecy and before as well as since their appointments had demonstrated an extraordinary degree of constant personal devotion to the

Governor and his wife. The Mansion penthouse was vast. It encompassed the Governor's official residence, state dining salons, guest apartments, gardens, two swimming pools. This small area was lost in its spaciousness, like a linen closet or a trunk room; its walls, ceilings, and floors were thoroughly soundproof, and the way into and out of it cunningly camouflaged.

"So you are now privy to my most heavily guarded state secret," smiled the Governor. "But from the first that was not a matter of concern to me since as you leave it I shall ask you to partake of a small glass of mulled cider in which will have been stirred a tasteless powder. This will affect you in one way and one only. After you drink it, you will have no memory of what you have seen and heard since you came in. I hope you won't mind."

"I shall mind very much indeed," said Grace. "But I suppose we should be thankful just to get out. You could be a modern Bluebeard."

"Oh, no," the Governor said comfortably. "Not at all. But a head of state must arrange for his own protection, and in my view he also has a right to a private life."

"We don't dispute that," Grace assured him. "And I certainly can't imagine being afraid of Beaver Wireman, especially since he wants to live like this in the middle of the twenty-first century. But what we really want to know is why you do. Also why it is of such paramount importance that it be kept a total secret."

The Governor said he was, himself, at a loss to explain why he and Sylvia had such a strong urge to live like this. Life would of course be infinitely easier for them if they didn't. Or should be. But the fact was that only here could he summon the qualities required for carrying out the duties of his office, and that if his wife stayed anywhere else than in this apartment for more than a few hours she became physically and emotionally ill. Until their youngest child had left for New State, when he came home from school on vacations they had of course had him come to the official residence and naturally Sylvia had tried to remain there as much as possible of his vacation time, yet increasingly she had to make excuses to slip away and rest here. Now that Dorian did not come and so she was spared this effort, though of course she missed him, her health was considerably improved.

He had no difficulty in recognizing the reason for the importance of secrecy in the matter, and felt no reluctance about giving it to them, since it would go no further. Indeed he did so with a great sense of relief, never having put it into words before. He and Sylvia had never spoken of it, even to each other; since she had not brought it up, he had not felt it wise that he should. But obviously their need of this particular kind of seclusion in an age and a world which had outgrown, discarded, destroyed, and forgotten it was an evidence of structural weakness, of some serious failure in the adjustment mechanism, of a sickness, if you will, which if it were known would be regarded as unfitting him for leadership of an enlightened nation.

"And perhaps rightly so," said the Governor. "Perhaps. But so far my observation and experience have convinced me that no one in Midway is without some weakness, some flaw which could make him unfit for great responsibility if, having been placed in a position of leadership, he proved incapable of self-analysis and self-discipline. I think I am capable of both, and that because my weakness is what it is and I can handle it as I do it does not endanger my country. I think I should know if it did, and I know that if I saw that it did I should resign my office immediately. I am not so certain that that would be true of Boulder Lee or Wool Freedland or anyone else."

"I see," Grace said slowly. "You feel

that your fellow countrymen could not understand their Governor's wanting to live like this, would not permit you to keep the office if they knew you live like this; yet you know that if you did not live like this – you and Sylvia – you could not appear to be what they believe you are or do what you and they consider the office requires."

"That's it. That's it exactly." The Governor rose and walked up and down. He stood before Grace, rubbing his palms on his trousers as if he were brushing off dust, and beamed down at her. "Why, I haven't talked this freely to anyone for more years than I care to count. And you understand it! Maybe you are my grandmother."

"I'm Beaver's grandmother, maybe," Grace said. "Not the Governor's, really. Not that man's in the white taffeta suit with all the purple cords and gold tassels posed in front of miles of purple velvet curtains. That's what Midway understands. At least, you imply that that – and all it apparently signifies – is what Midway understands, and I have to take your word for it. But this is what George and I understand, and what Beaver Wireman and his wife understand, and we are the only people here, as all by ourselves as if we were in one of the little old country houses in Old State, a half-mile deep in the woods and a mile from the nearest neighbor. It's been a very interesting evening. Now I'll take my candle and climb the creaky stairs. You wake up George and see he takes off his pants before he gets into bed. Goodnight, Beaver."

But before she closed her bedroom door she called back softly, "What about those dishes? Did you put them to soak?"

The Governor chuckled.

"Keep on up your creaky stairs, Gram. Before I go to bed I'll touch a button, a curtain in the ballroom will move in a specified place in a specified way, and Fern will see it because she will be watching for it. She will be over soon after that to tidy the kitchen and plump up the cushions. Fern is Sylvia's secretary."

George, roused, had heard this. He was looking at his watch.

"Odd job for a secretary, seems like. Odd working hours for a girl, too."

The Governor laughed aloud.

"The 'girl' is used to it. She's been doing it for five years now. There are ample rewards."

"Oh, I don't doubt what you say. Seems to me everything in this state is more'n ample."

The next morning as Grace was leaving the bathroom there was a light tap on its other door. She turned and looked at it.

"Miss Murkle? Are you ready for your breakfast tray?"

The voice was so low Grace almost doubted she had heard it at all. Besides, an answer required some thought. What did it mean in Midway to be ready for a breakfast tray? In Old State it meant to be sick-a-bed but have a little appetite.

"Miss Murkle? I hope I'm not disturbing you. You are awake?"

"Oh, yes. Wide awake. But I thought I'd take a bath."

This was the first opportunity she had seen since leaving home, and the way one thing kept running into another it might be the last until she got back there.

"Oh, of course. But won't you please just hop back into bed afterward? I want to bring your tray."

"Well, thanks. But don't go to any trouble. I can perfectly well – "

"Oh, it's no trouble. I love to fix trays and there's never anybody who wants one. Beaver likes to make his own breakfast and when the children used to come from school they hated staying in bed a minute after they woke up. If they were sick they had to be sent straight off to the infirmary."

'I'll be back in bed in ten minutes," Grace promised.

"Oh, thank you, Miss Murkle."

Grace thought, "And here we are back in Wonderland; I feel as if I'm Alice, but probably she is; if she is, who is Sylvia, where is Beaver, and if George is awake, what is he making of it?"

The Wiremans' tub was of a size and shape familiar to her. The soap was white and clean-smelling. The towels were white and absorbent but not heavy. Her bath was very satisfactory. When she returned to her room a lacy lavender bed jacket with narrow black velvet ribbon run through the insertion lay on the pillows which had been increased in number and heaped invitingly against the tufted headboard. She put on the jacket, sat upright against the pillows, folded her hands, and waited.

Whatever she expected, it was not what came.

A wicker tea cart painted sun yellow with a high gloss and topped by polished white linen and a small conservatory was wheeled in by the Greek concept of a goddess in human form – a woman some six feet tall with a sturdy body, long arms and legs, long slender feet, big, capable hands, broad shoulders, strong, full neck, and massive head. The whole outline of the figure was plainly visible though wrapped in a loose-fitting robe of clear blue cotton. The beautiful feet were bare. And the face . . . every feature was classic and on a grand scale; square chin, wide, bowed mouth, high cheekbones, generous nose, enormous purple eyes, big, perfect ears and white brow from which red-gold hair streaked with silver was drawn back tightly into an enormous coil at the back of her neck.

Surely she could not be the person who had spoken through the bathroom door? She must have a voice like a church organ, perhaps communicated only through music. Even Grace felt it would be effrontery to speak first. She sat frankly staring.

"Good morning, dear Miss Murkle! I'm Sylvia Wireman. Oh, I forgot to run up this shade. I'm so sorry. There, now you can see what a lovely morning it is. Are you quite comfortable there? If you are, I have this little table to put across your knees. See, it has a special little clamp to hold your flower vase so it can't tip and get you all wet. I brought sweet peas. I hope you like them. I know you like roses because one was pinned to your coat in the closet. I took it off to refresh it. I hope you don't mind. I popped it into very hot water for a bit, and then into cold, and back and forth. I think it helped a little, but the poor thing must have had quite a dreadful experience in that stuffy closet without water all night. I suppose you were so tired you forgot it. Now here's your juice. I made it myself from our own tangerines. I'll just put your plants on the windowsills. This is a Pink Lady geranium and this is a Star of Bethlehem. These sills are their home, really, but I always take them out at night. I tell Beaver plants need to sleep alone. These were slipped from plants that were slips from plants I brought with me when I came to Midway. I think they are my most precious possessions. Your rose is so lovely. I have it in the refrigerator now. I do hope it revives. I have a strange feeling I've seen some like it, but if I did it was a long, long time ago and if I did I can't understand why I didn't try to take the bush with me. Maybe I did try. Maybe they wouldn't let me. Or maybe it didn't survive the transplanting. So much doesn't, I find; and that seems to me such a pity. I shouldn't, I know. Let me pour your coffee. I think it must be cooled just enough to drink. You sit and sip it and look at the sweet peas and the plants on the sunny windowsill. I expect you're still very tired and need quiet. I'll be back in one minute with the rest of your breakfast. . . ."

Grace had just time to realize that this was indeed the voice of an organ but one with faulty bellows, sternly muted, and played at a great distance; then it and its user returned bringing fresh coffee, feathery hot muffins, and strawberry preserves.

"Would you like to be by yourself for breakfast? Or are you rested enough now so that you would enjoy some conversation with it? Do tell me honestly. I want everything to be just as you want it, dear Miss Murkle. I want you to be perfectly happy here. I'll do whatever you wish. Please tell me what it is. You see, I – "

There was no other way than to interrupt her.

"Of course I'll tell you, Sylvia. First, I wish you not to call me Miss Murkle. Lately I seemed to be everybody's grandmother, and I'd like for you to call me that or any derivative or diminutive thereof. Second – "

"Oh, Miss – no, oh, may I call you Granny? I think – I've always thought – "

"Yes, call me Granny if you like. That's a bit of a change again. Second, if you want me to relax – rest, as you call it – I must know where George is. He would hate it, and I try to conceal it, but while we are away from home I feel responsible for him. He is eighty years old, and – ”

“George?”

“Everybody’s grandfather. You are probably still calling him – ”

“Oh, Mr. Peterson! I haven’t had the pleasure of meeting him yet. Beaver insisted on making his breakfast, and they are together in the kitchen. Quite early. And then they went out. I know where they went because I eavesdropped. It was so exciting to hear Beaver talking with another man the way he talks with Mr. Peterson. So freely. I’ve never heard him talking like that with anyone since we came to Midway and he began working in the government. I suppose you can’t when you’re Governor. Or getting ready to be. Unless to a very exceptional person. So Mr. Peterson must be a most exceptional – ”

“But where is he?”

“Oh, I suppose he is in the gardens by now. Beaver was going to show him the

Top Ballroom where the reception is going to be held tonight, and the official guestrooms where he will be staying after the reception. Then Beaver had to go to the office, and Mr. Peterson was going to visit the gardens until Beaver comes back to have lunch with him. If Mr. Peterson loves flowers as he must – he sounds like such a dear **man – he can easily spend all morning in the gardens, for they are very large. So we should find him there unless of course he has grown tired and gone to his room to rest. Shall we look?"**

"Later, maybe, If we can do it without seeming to. It would never do for George to suspect that I'm following him around. If you're satisfied that that's where he is – "

"Oh, I'm quite **sure, but let's verify it. That would make you easier in your mind, wouldn't it? I want you to be perfectly easy in your mind today, dear – Granny. And it probably won't take a minute. I'll just open my garden window. Beaver was so good to have it**

made for me. Beaver is wonderfully kind to me. He knows I couldn't live long where I couldn't see the gardens, any and all parts of them, any time I like."

She touched a button and a small wall panel flew back revealing what at first appeared to be a rectangular window opening on a garden of almost unearthly luxuriance but quickly became more like a television screen as Sylvia turned a knob, not to change channels, but to tour that fabulous view slowly as one might walk through it, to penetrate its shadowy areas as with a strong searchlight, to pick out and enlarge a particular blossom or leaf or stone or butterfly or tiny waterfall as with a high-powered telescope.

"Not – really!" Grace exclaimed.

But there, unquestionably, were George's hindquarters and the soles of his shoes. A slight movement of the knob – this must, Grace thought, require a skill rather like that needed for driving a car, except that you could not run into anyone, nor anyone into you – brought the two women around – or did it bring George around? – to where Grace could see that he was down on all fours under a bush in the part of this Paradise soberly sticking his tongue into one cupped hand.

"This must be Mr. Peterson," cried Sylvia. "But whatever is he doing, dear – Granny?"

"That is Mr. Peterson," Grace replied, and drank thirstily from her coffee cup. "And what he is doing, he is tasting the soil of the Mansion gardens." She piled strawberry jam on a muffin and bit into it hungrily. "That's your grandfather, my dear."

"But why does he do that?"

"To find out what's in it. If he can."

"Oh, I'm not sure he should! But of course if there were anything in it that would poison him, the gardeners would have told him. Two of them are just on the other side of that bush."

Sylvia barely touched her knob, George vanished, and two men came into view who looked exactly like Slipper's and Sparrow's escorts of the night before except that they were wearing only flowered shorts and each held a long metal strip that must be some new fangled type of garden tool. They were staring downward, presumably at George, and completely expressionless.

"If they did tell him it might poison him," said Grace, "he probably said if it would poison him it wouldn't produce plants like that, and went right ahead with his tasting."

"But if it would they would have stopped him."

"I'm glad they didn't feel they had to try. George is a very stubborn man, and the one thing I don't want is for anybody to accuse us of being the cause of any more interstate incidents, at least until we've cleared up the first one. . . . Thanks, Sylvia. Now you can turn off or shut down whatever it is, if you want to. I'm ready for that conversation you proposed some little time ago."

"Oh, – are you sure? I don't want to hurry you. We do have all day, you know. Until we have to be dressed for the reception. But only this one day. Beaver said very distinctly that this one day is all we'll have alone together. But he did promise me that. Nobody is going to disturb us. And he promised me something else that he has never promised me before and that I've never had with anyone since we came to Midway, if I ever did. He told me I could say anything to you I wanted to – if you didn't mind – and that it would be all right. I needn't worry about it, whatever it was. I needn't even think about it. it would be perfectly all right."

Grace could figure out how that was. She had not forgotten the promise of mulled cider which he had made to her, and was not likely to.

"If he told you so, then of course it is," she said. "So let's begin. You say whatever you want to. When I've sat here long enough I'll dress and we'll go out to the living room – because there's a limit to how long I can stay in one place late years – but you keep right on with our conversation."

"Well," said Sylvia, sliding back in her chair, eagerness spreading like a light all over her, "first I want to tell you a great many things. Then I want to ask you a great many things."

She wanted to tell her life story. She had been born in what was now Old State but could remember nothing specific about it, only a generalized feeling of being surrounded by a constant tenderness which she had an aching longing to return in kind or perhaps to extend to some who would welcome it from her as she welcomed it from others. She was an only child at the time, because complications at her birth – "Among other things, I later learned, I was a very large baby, especially for a firstborn" – had resulted in a long period of invalidism for her mother. This may also have been the reason that she and her parents lived with her mother's parents, as did her mother's young sisters and brother. Sylvia was four years old when the present division of Great Country was made, and this household was of course soon scattered in all directions. Sylvia could remember nothing about the leave-taking or who left first, but had been told later that two college-age aunts and an uncle had gone in joyful haste to the dormitories just completed in New State, and that her father had been perhaps fully as eager to get his little family under his own roof in Two State. So it may have been that the grandparents had been the ones to close the old family homestead, before flying to Midway and putting their youngest daughter in school here.

"There is one other impression I still have of North State, as it was called when we lived there. I wish it were clearer. I spend a great deal of time trying to get it into focus. Last night I lay awake wondering if possibly you could help me. Try to think, Granny, if there is anything still there that I would recognize if I could go back – that I may recognize when I do go back – that would make a small child, if a small child were there, feel that there was somebody she couldn't see and nobody else could see but who sometimes spoke to her and gave her something – something very big; well, not big, maybe, but very important. Something she had to have, and nobody else could give to her, and that she couldn't get for herself. . . . Something that this is somehow instead of, or maybe even part of. Or anyway it is the nearest to it that I have now."

She opened a door off the bedroom. The room it led to was long and narrow with bare white walls. It was just large enough for a cot, with a walkway beside it.

"Lit down there, can you, Granny? Lie on your back. Just for a minute."

Grace lay there. The ceiling was one pane of glass. The touch of a button opened this window; another touch closed it. Open or closed, it revealed a piece of the sky.

Sylvia said Beaver had not at all understood why she asked to have this in the apartment. She was not sure herself, only that she needed it. Nor did he know how much time she spent in it. She felt that if he did he would worry about it. But he had told her she was free to say whatever she wanted to say today.

She had much clearer memories of Two State than of North State, of course. Two sets of them. So different that they were almost like the memories of two people. As a child in Two State she had encountered loneliness for the first time. It had never since entirely left her – and for many years now she had known that everyone must live with and endure it in varying degrees – but in the same period that it was new to her it had been almost total. She had been removed from the only home, the only landscape she had ever known and from all but two of the people who had been her world until then. The new house was very small and very quiet. Her father seemed to her to be nearly always away and her mother, when not away with him, nearly always resting. When she asked them about going home they said, "Someday." When she asked if they were going to see Grandfather again, Granny, Uncle Bill, the Aunties, they said, "Maybe." Ever since then she had wanted to run away and hide whenever anyone said, "Someday," or "Maybe."

Gradually, things had changed for Sylvia in Two State. She grew old enough to go to school. She was so much larger than the other children in the beginning class and somehow knew so much that they didn't know that she suddenly had a wildly happy feeling. She thought the time had come when she could be to little children and do for little children what others had been to her and done for her when she was a little child. But her classmates did not understand. They were afraid of her. They ran away, leaving her alone in a corner of the school grounds, holding out her arms. The teachers put her in a class of larger children and then in a class of still larger children until she realized that they were too big, that the time really had not come for her to be happy and maybe never would. All there was for her was the library. She was always finishing a book and being given another book.

At last she was nine years old and her mother never seemed to be resting any more. Her mother had pink cheeks and high black boots and skirts as short as Sylvia's and went dancing and to meetings and was going to have a baby and right after that did have a baby. The first time Sylvia saw that baby – little Rob – she again had that wildly happy feeling; so happy and so wild this time that it frightened her because it was so strong and she was so alone with it.

"What ever that was I had in North State and whatever it gave me didn't go with me to Two State. I never had anything but the longing for it until Beaver gave me my sky window six years ago. And I still don't know what it was, Granny."

She wanted to do for Rob, but they told her he was too little. When she asked to hold him, they said, "Someday," and if, when it was time, she could help him to walk, they said, "Maybe." So she ran away in tears and hid with the books, and somehow before Someday came, or Maybe, it was decided that she was ready for Midway schools.

"I couldn't begin to understand it then, the day they packed my things, the day they put me on the plane. I suppose I understand it now. I had completed the Two State school curriculum. As I learned later, my mother was pregnant again. Now that she was well they were starting a new family which would keep them in Two State for a long time. When I came to Midway I would have to come alone, and if I came at that time my grandparents would be here for me to spend vacations with. They told me this and expected me to understand, but I didn't. They did not tell me I might never see them again, but I think I knew

I wouldn't."

Her grandparents met the plane in Midway, but either she had forgotten nearly everything about them in those six Two State years or they had greatly changed. Probably both. At first sight of them she was frightened by the signs of their age. She could still remember that when her grandfather came toward her reaching for her hand she thrust her hands into her pockets, and when her grandmother would have kissed her she drew back. They never tried to touch her again. They drove her directly to the school where she had been registered and was expected. They gave the headmaster their names, their telephone number, and their relationship to the new pupil, then said a polite goodbye to Sylvia and went away. Both at school and later by them in vacation time, she was told that it was best to form close relationships only with contemporaries as she would be associated with those older or younger only for brief periods.

The shock of losing their family had apparently been shattering to her grandparents. Her grandfather told her that her grandmother had never recovered from it and never would. Though this generational separation had been in the planning stage for many years before it was finalized and official, and was even during that period being practiced by many, they had assumed that it could not happen to a family as close-knit as theirs. But for six years now no word had reached them from their Luna, Dorothea, or Bill in New State; or from Lisa in the two years since she went there, though during the four years Lisa had been in school in Midway – as Sylvia was now – they had clung to her as their only reason for being, and lived from one of her vacations to the next. Sylvia could remember her grandfather's haunted eyes as he said, "We have had our lesson. We shall not put on you the burden we may have put on Lisa, nor get ourselves in the way of another such blow as losing her was for us. In these incredible times, one learns that what he does not have he cannot lose." They did not even ask her questions about their daughter Merry and her family in Two State, but seemed to have resolved to live in the present, entertaining and being entertained by people like themselves, playing bridge, taking drives, watching the tube. Sylvia had been thirteen when word reached her at school that she would now be spending her vacations at Cranberry Lodge, one of many pupil resorts maintained by the Midway school system, as her grandfather had reached retirement age and he and her grandmother had that day been flown to Old State. She could not now recall having had any reaction to that news. She was alone, but no more so than she had long been and expected always to be, associated almost exclusively with those with whom she would be associated as long as she lived and with not one of whom she had formed a close relationship. She did not know why, since many of them did form such relationships. To her they all seemed too big. Still she was always bigger than they. It was bewildering.

At the age of fifteen she had completed the preparatory school courses and was sent to New State.

"I have very little recollection of any but my last year in New State. When I try to remember the earlier ones I am swept by horror. I hope you have no wish to visit there."

"Oh, yes," said Grace cheerfully. "We do wish to, and we intend to. That was in the contract. We are expected to report back to Old State on all its sister states."

"Oh, Granny, dear! . . . Well, perhaps it is greatly improved by now. I try to believe so, since both our children are there. Or perhaps even then it was not so dreadful as I think. Beaver has always told me it wasn't. He got on very well there. But Beaver seems to get on well anywhere. I wonder what the effect on both of us would have been if we had met sooner."

For Sylvia, Two State had compounded loneliness and bewilderment with terror. Her teachers were machines and great, arched, echoing libraries. There was nothing else but torn-up pavements, ragged, muddy parks greasy coffeehouses and bars, dirty shops, dirty apartments, dirty pots, dirty paper, dirty beds, and throngs of strange, sad, dirty, shivering or sweating creatures dragging themselves from one place to another, one beastly, boring game to another. Her only conscious wish was to escape all she was engulfed in, but for a long time there was not even a gleam of hope that she could. She did not expect to live to be thirty and go back to Two State, nor have any desire to. That was too long to wait here even for something that she wanted very much. And she remembered nothing about Two State that she wanted to recover except its cleanliness, which she had no reason to suppose still existed, since every week more New Staters were flown up there to become its citizenry and take it over.

More and more she stayed in the libraries, hiding in their dark recesses from the decreasing number who left the lobbies and corridors, where they crowded to sleep and eat and drink, and wandered into the front of the stack-rooms. Gradually she learned that some libraries were safer than others, either because they had deeper recesses or were less conveniently situated. Finally she found one with both advantages and made it her home. In the semi-basement there was a lavatory and shower off a storage room. She cleaned out the storage room, swept it with a broom, scrubbed it top and bottom and all around with mops and brushes and rags discovered in a closet. At first she slept on a blanket there, but as time went on she brought in one by one a folding cot, pieces of linoleum to cover the floor, a propane gas grate, a few odd dishes, the frames of chairs which had once been upholstered. She scrubbed everything she brought in and for weeks scrubbed it all again every few days. Then she got material, washed it, dried it in early morning sunshine – there was never anyone about in the early mornings – and made herself sheets, towels, coverlets, cushions, and clothing. She was always washing either her possessions or herself; she shampooed her hair every night for months, took at least two showers a day.

"I was mad about water. Water – and soap. Soap and water.... In a way I still am. I think I'll always be. Dirt is so ugly."

In her early twenties she was the most content she had ever been within her memory; no longer aware of loneliness, for that condition rests on the assumption that one is cut off from a person or persons, or perhaps a place, with whom or where he longs to be. Sylvia had learned to want only to escape, and she had done so. She was as alone as if she were the only human being alive. Those she saw on the streets and in the shops and at the bank, when she stole out disguised in the stained pants, hooded, torn jacket, and runover boots she kept beside the storage room door for these rare excursions, seemed far less her own kind than the thin dogs and sick cats that prowled the alleys and pawed and scratched among the empty cans and littered papers.

Then suddenly there was Beaver.

Slipping in through her back door at dusk one evening, she found she could not close it. Looking back to see why, she looked into his smiling face.

She had never seen him before. Her throat rusty from disuse, she asked him what he wanted.

"I want to talk to you."

"Go away, please. I have nothing to say to you."

"I think you have. Anyway, I'm going to ask you some questions. May I come in?"

"No."

"I'm coming in.... This is really better, you know. If you don't even want me, you certainly don't want a crowd. And a crowd is what you'd have got it you'd kept me standing outside. Because I don't stand anywhere long without a crowd gathering. . . . There are better libraries than this if you have a thing about libraries. Why do you say here so much?"

"What makes you think I do?"

"I know you do. I know something about you. I know your name is Sylvia Tennant. I know you are twenty-two years old. I know you buy different things than most people buy, and that you bring them here; which in itself is intriguing."

"I don't know anything about you and I don't want to. Please go away."

"If I went away now, I'd be back later. If I stay a while now, I may never come back. Isn't it better to get me over with sooner rather than later? If you really want to get me over with? . . . I have a suspicion you live in this library, Sylvia Tennant."

"It's none of your business where I

live."

"But I'm curious. I'm a curious kind of man. Why would anybody want to live in a library?"

"Why do you want to live wherever you live?"

"I don't, especially. I just happen to have stopped there. But I thought everybody lived where other people lived. You certainly don't. I've followed you a dozen times before this and you never go where other people live. You never even stop where other people are. You always come straight back here. I'm not sure you are people."

"Neither am I. What does that have to do with anything?"

"Everything. Because if you are you're a different kind. That's exciting enough. But if you aren't, what are you? That's even more exciting."

Well, that was Beaver Wireman. So what else could have happened than that in a little while she opened the door of the sotrage room to him, and herself went to the shower to get out of her street clothes, bathe, and put on a clean cotton dress and sandals before coming back to sit opposite him and listen to his questions? She was surprised by the number that she answered honestly that night. Other nights she answered the rest, and more, and asked many of her own. She found that he was indeed a person, and not altogether unlike herself, though he had lived comfortably and with enjoyment in an environment unendurable for her. He found that she, too, was a person, one new to his experience and one who not only intrigued him but challenged and inspired him, the first woman he had known whom he could fully admire, the woman he loved. She now redicovered loneliness, for whenever he was not there she was lonely. But he was there many nights during the year that followed. They were married in the only way marriage took place in New State – by promising each other that they would be married as soon as they reached Two State. However, this was their secret.

He continued his work at the bank, his study of law, his social life, both because he enjoyed them and because, as he explained to her, their future depended on them. She went on living exactly as she had for so long except that now he was the secret center of her life, and this was an all-encompassing exception. She gave her full time to preparing, under his direction, for the brand-new and glorious life which lay ahead. She read what he told her to read, made constant improvements in the household items to which they were now both so attached that they were resolved to have them shipped to Two State if he could find any possible way, and a month before they were to go there went alone to the hospital like any other pregnant girl in New State and had her baby. The hospital was a dreadful place, as she had known it would be, and though she left it with the baby when he was only two days old he had contracted an eye infection which left him sightless.

But this had not been the tragedy to

Sylvia, at the time, that she later found it to be. She had her baby. Someday had come. No one could ever again put her off with Maybe. Beaver left for Two State one week. She and the baby followed him the next. He met her plane. Their home was waiting for them, and their own familiar furnishings were in it. Beaver, being Beaver, had contrived to manage that. They had a justice of the peace to dinner, with his wife, and when he had married them legally, Beaver, the judge, and the judge's wife Marigold undertook to teach Sylvia to play bridge. The house was new and clean, Beaver was wearing a shirt and tie and new jacket not unlike the judge's, and Marigold was neat and pretty. Sylvia made fresh coffee later and brought out a box of little cakes she had made that morning and brought with her on the plane. It was all beautiful. It all seemed perfectly natural.

After that everything had been beautiful and natural for a long time.

They had another child the next year. Another boy. She had wanted a little girl very much, but soon learned she had been most fortunate to have a second child at all, as some damage from the birth of the first was irreparable and step had to be taken immediately to prevent her ever becoming pregnant again. Still everything seemed beautiful to her, and grew more so. She had two babies and a man of her own on whom to lavish the flood of tenderness which, having been dammed up so long, was rushing out. She and Beaver were every day more in love, and his law practice was in high gear. He was enormously popular and deeply respected and gloried in every minute of it. Sylvia found such happiness in watching his happiness that she wanted to go out with him, and through going out with him she found herself liked and admired, too. Most people seemed a little in awe of them; they laughed about this when they were at home by themselves, living with their familiar comforts, playing with their little boys. But Beaver said it might be a good thing, probably an asset, and so it seemed to be. As Beaver conceived of many improvements which could be made in Two State institutions and rallied his followers to bring them about, Sylvia was elected to school and hospital boards and went up the ladder to the state presidency of the Women's Union. So that when he was appointed Governor of Two State and she became its First Lady this seemed logical and natural to them and to everyone else. They continued to live in their own home, very much as they had before. There was little formality in Two State. Everyone's chief concern there was with the welfare of the children, and a way of life built around children is likely to be simple and wholesome.

Oh, the Two State years were good years for the Wiremans. But they passed so fast!

Though Toolie was very bright, his blindness did keep him from advancing as fast scholastically as he otherwise would have. He was fourteen when he completed the requirements of the Two State school system, and he and Dorian were graduated together. As it was necessary then for them to go to Midway and their father had another year to serve in his Two State office, Sylvia had gone alone to Midway with the boys. Because Beaver understood what a wrench this separation and change was for Sylvia, and because of Toolie's problem, he had used his influence to arrange that the boys could stay with her that first year, going in to school only for classes and returning home each day when classes were over – Toolie so that he could have his mother's help in ways he was accustomed to, and Dorian to be man-of-the-house for both of them.

"This was our first mistake," said Sylvia. "Oh, Granny, dear, I've talked right through the morning, and through lunch, and now I'm afraid it's getting very close to the time when Fern will come to get us ready for the reception.

Or maybe Beaver will come to take us over to the official apartments and Fern will come there to get us ready for the reception. I forget how Beaver planned that. Or maybe he didn't tell me. But it is getting late, and I haven't asked you any of all the questions I wanted to ask you about Old State! I do want so much to know! And there were things I wanted to show you. I'm afraid, too, I've tired you. You should have a chance to rest. But I must tell you what – what – "

"What life has been like since you came to Midway," Grace said. She touched Sylvia's hand. It was ice cold. "Since you came with Toolie and Dorian. Tell me."

Sylvia should have waited for Beaver, or Beaver should have resigned his Two State office and gone to Midway with his family. But above all the boys should have proceeded precisely within the system, like all other children. Fortunately for Beaver later, very few Midway adults knew that they didn't, for Sylvia made no friends or even acquaintances that year, living only with and for the boys; and by the time Beaver was there to begin renewing old friendships and making new ones, Toolie and Dorian were permanently placed in school. But their fellow-students saw them as strangers, interlopers, and nothing the Wireman boys ever did changed their image basically. Toolie was stricken by his non-acceptance. From a dark, warm sweet cocoon he had been cast into dark, frigid waters. His first vacations at home were filled with heartbreaking revelations of his misery and with pleading to be helped out of those waters. As years went on he said less and less until he hardly spoke at all, often did not answer when spoken to. Dorian reacted differently. Realizing – as Toolie did not, fully – in that first year that he was in an impossible situation, Dorian had placed the blame for it entirely on his parents and become very difficult for Sylvia to manage. She had seen one flash of the old lively, warmhearted Dorian when his father came – the father he so closely resembled – and he had gone of to school jubilant, sure that when he lived as his contemporaries lived he would make his place among them. But apparently he was never allowed to do this. He had missed his one opportunity. He had not been there last year. He was a year late. So while Toolie turned inward and nursed his suffering as his mother had, Dorian struck out in all directions as his father would have in his place – difficult as it was to conceive of Beaver ever having been in such a place. Dorian despised his brother and all others he considered to be weak, including his mother. He soon came to hate his father, his teachers, and all others who were in positions of authority or displayed qualities of strength. Everyone who knew Dorian had reason to fear him, and did. In a conscientious effort to make something of him, Midway school authorities, with Beaver's approval (for by then Beaver was Governor of

Midway and Chief Administrative Officer of Great Country), kept Dorian for two years after Toolie was sent to New State – "Oh, Granny, dear, whatever has become of Toolie there?" – but it did no good; quite otherwise; his earlier "scrapes" were escalating into crimes, so in despair they gave him up.

The day each fall when planes left Midway to take that year's contingent to New was known as Off-to-College Day, not only a full-scale state holiday but the one most extravagantly celebrated there except Inauguration which occurred only once each decade. The night before Off-to-College there were parties everywhere, even in the streets, with millions of colored lights, the sky filled with exploding fireworks, snake dancing with blazing torches, free food and drinks on every corner. Parents were notified of the time and port from which their boy or girl would be leaving. As the sun rose, it found every port massed with flowers, strung with white satin ribbons, draped with school banners, and banners bearing slogans, rocking with music, and with every rooftop and every pole – there as throughout Midway – flying the Great Country flag. At endless white-covered tables leading citizens – men in white suits and women in fabulous gowns – were serving youth its choice of all known breakfast menus – rare fresh fruits and just-squeezed juices, hot muffins as richly stuffed as holiday puddings, pancakes and waffles with syrup (twenty-some varieties), eggs cooked as-you-like-them, smoking bacon, sizzling sausages, ham with watercress, and foods of which Sylvia did not even yet know the name.

Then one after another the planes were announced over the loudspeakers, and Midway boys and girls swarmed out and up the ramps. As each plane was filled its door closed and the ramp was pushed away.

Sylvia never felt that she was going to be able to go to the next Off-to-College Day, but she always did. She had to. She was the Governor's wife.

It was years now since she had seen even one girl or boy look back and wave toward the pavilions where all their parents stood. Officials and those who had come only for the fun were not admitted to the pavilions and saw the departures from a distance, hazily, but each parent was given the use of an exceptional pair of field glasses made especially for this purpose. Through it he could follow his son or daughter closely and exclusively all the way to his or her seat in the plane and to that extent stay with him until the plane moved beyond its range.

"Sometimes I forget it for weeks," Sylvia said slowly. "What I saw through my glasses from the pavilion in my turn. Then it comes back and I don't understand how I could ever forget it for an instant. My Toolie, in the crimson uniform of his school, slumped in that blue velvet seat, his sightless eyes seeming to stare at his bare hands which were locked together so tightly that I could see how white his knuckles were and how the veins stood out. . . . And two years later my Dorian, in his crimson uniform, first twisting around to look provocatively, threateningly at his fellow-passengers and then suddenly putting his sneering young face close to the window to grin evilly at his father and me – of course he couldn't see us but – but he looked as if he could – and spit on the glass. . . . So the last I ever saw of my two children was Dorian's – Dorian's – "

Sylvia Wireman, born Tennant, fell sidelong on the sofa where she had been sitting, and was racked by sobs.

A few minutes later the Governor came hurrying in and bent over her.

"What is it? Sylvia, why are you crying so? What is the matter?. . . Sylvia, my darling! Sylvia – "

She sat up and stared at him. When he tried to put his arms around her, she pushed him away.

"I was remembering," she said hoarsely. "Do you remember, too? I must know if you remember it too. The day they took Toolie away. And that other day. The day Dorian ... Dorian – "

Grace saw the cords in the Governor's neck above his collar.

"I never think of it," he said. "You must not think of it, darling. I'll get you something right away that will help you. You will rest then. You will sleep and forget."

He hurried out of the room.

"Come," Grace said to Sylvia. "Come with me quickly. Come in here and look up at your sky. Up there is what you told me about that used to come to you when you were little and give you something very important, something no one else had for you. It is still there, Sylvia. Up is the place to look for it, to reach for it. It is Spirit, Sylvia. The Great Spirit. In Old State we call it God. You can reach Him if you try. Believe me, Sylvia. He is there and He can help you."

She closed the door and was standing

with her back against it when the Governor returned.

She said gently, "If you love her, let her cry, Beaver. Let her remember. She must remember or you will lose her entirely. And if you lose her, you will lose everything."

For a minute they faced each other squarely. Then he looked away and his breath came roughly.

He said, "If you are – sure of that – you know more about me than anyone else does. Even her. For she – sometimes – doubts it. But to me – she is everything. Everything."

"I only suspected that. Though I strongly suspected it. But I meant more. Not only your own reason for going on, but all that depends on you right now. The whole future of this – this tortured country you hold the reins of."

"What do you mean? What has she told you?"

"Much that I don't think she had ever thought through before. Much that she did not know she was telling me. Sit down, Beaver. I must talk to you. Then George and I must leave for New State as quickly as we can. There will be nothing more we can do here. Whatever is done here you must do."

She told him that his wife had confirmed her worst fears of what this diabolical division of Great Country by generations was doing to its citizens, hadvery nearly completed and made irrevocable. It was bad enough for everyone's active years to lead only to oblivion, isolation, a long, useless waiting for death; a prospect horrible enough in itself to make those closest to it – the middle-aged of Midway – be inseparable from their Be-Bes, crave his Whizzers, and have no objection to taking his mulled cider if prescribed. Bad enough for little children to grow up with no knowledge of God, no grandparents to turn to, no other resource than what could be provided by those who, after leaving Midway as lost creatures filled with hate and despair, had spent a dozen years or more in the lawless, hopeless slum that New State apparently was. Still, by comparison, and in view of Sylvia's testimony, Two State was now the Paradise of Great Country. Little children knew nothing of hate and a great deal about love, and parents could still love their children. No wonder the parents, more or less remembering what lay behind them – and ahead of their children – were darkly suspicious of and bitterly belligerent toward everything beyond their borders, and increasingly on the verge of revolution against the system. So they should be. And they would revolt. This was one of the messages she had brought here for him and would take home to Old State.

"I knew a revolution was coming, Beaver. I knew that before long Two State would rise up against Midway and, realizing how little they had to fight with, compared with what you had, I came to plead with you to try to avoid any violent confrontation, at least to postpone it, at the very least to make it abortive and give first priority to setting up meetings with Governor Hurd and his staff and opening avenues by which those young people could get information about and experience in the operation of national government. Of all our ways of life in this country, theirs is the simplest, and, as Sylvia said, the most natural. They have not yet been participants in complication, only the victims of it."

But from what she had seen and heard here, she knew now that Midway, for all its trappings of power, was a clock running down and its key misplaced, or a machine wearing out from long use without proper greasing or the required replacement of parts. Midway, apparently without knowing it was in far greater need of immediate revolution than Two State felt itself to be.

"You know it, Beaver. It's no use to deny it. Why should you want to deny it? All you have here is what is left of your people. They are sick from feeding so long off themselves, from having been cast out at the age of twelve or thirteen to inhabit a wilderness, from never knowing anything better than Two State and that so temporarily, from not daring to look forward or back, from not being allowed the comfort of attachment, from having their lives – every single one of them – sharply broken off at regular, set intervals. . . . It is ghastly. Even more ghastly than I thought. . . . You are all hollow. You are all sick. Even you, Beaver Wireman. But you are not dead. You are not, most of you, even dying. It's very late, but it isn't too late. Start the revolution. You can do it, you and Sylvia. You are the only ones with the strength and the authority to start one and make it successful."

"Sylvia – the strength?"

"Oh, Sylvia is very strong. How, being the warm sensitive, idealistic person she is, has she managed to stay warm, sensitive, idealistic, and heart-stoppingly beautiful through all that has happened to her since this miserable, doomed experiment began when she was four years old? By being too strong to be defeated by it. Just as you were and are. And by having a source of strength she didn't know she had. As I think you must have, too. And if you two have, many others must have. But every day the lines of communication with what we all used to know grow thinner. There is no time to lose."

He was not listening. He had gone to Sylvia's door and tapped.

She opened it and smiled out at him, reached for his hand.

"Is it time to dress for the reception, dear?"

"There's no hurry. Do you feel like going to a reception?"

"Oh, of course. I think I must have slept a few minutes. I feel fine." She came out. There was a soft glow all over her. She put her arm around Grace. "How about you, Granny, dear? Have you rested at all?"

"I didn't need to," Grace assured

her. "I never sleep in the daytime."

"Then while we're changing," said the Governor, "I'll have our dinner brought over here and ask Gramp to come along. He was going to change in the apartment there, and I'd thought we'd eat in the state dining room with the guys and dolls. But why don't we four stay here where we can talk? They'll never miss us."

"Oh, how nice!" Sylvia said happily. "Granny, show me what you will wear to the reception and I'll choose something to match."

They spent two hours over dinner, and stood an hour in the receiving line at the reception during which the Governor was very jovial and his lady even more than usually stunning. Some grumbling was overheard about the Whizzers seeming weak, but in general the Midwayans concentrated on the odd little visitors whom the Governor introduced as "our neighbors from Old State who have accorded us the courtesy of stopping over with us on their way home after supervising the safe return to Two State of the young boys who had been lost on Great Mountain." When George was asked if it seemed good to see Midway again he said well, he couldn't say it felt much like home, they had made so many changes in it since he left; but one thing he was curious about was why the stems of their plants were getting so thick and hard, while the blossoms were smaller than in Old State and didn't have as much smell, so he was going to dig up a few to take home with him and see how they worked out in that soil over there. When Grace was asked if she would come to an annual convention at which the officers of Midway women's organizations were meeting and give a talk on what life was like in Old State, she said if they would invite her to their next convention she would make every effort to come, but her visit this time was too brief; they were to leave in the morning for New State.

At this response all eyes turned to the Governor.

They would come back another year? They were going to New State?

Sylvia, her arm around Grace, said, "Oh, I wish as much as you do we could keep them longer. It seems to me almost like getting my own grandparents back. You know, I remember my grandparents. I suppose many of you don't. But they will come back. I'm sure they will. They simply must. There is so much we want to talk with them about. After all, first thing we know, we'll be going over there to live with them and we should be getting acquainted, shouldn't we?"

The Governor, with a hand on George's shoulder, said, "Yes, we've urged them to stay a while but they remind me that they aren't used to being long away from home. This has been rather a strenuous trip but they tell me they've found it very interesting and we're pleased about that. We're going to take them back to their rooms now before they get overtired. By the way, any of you who would like to send messages to your children in New State, just write them out before you go tonight, with the name attached, and leave them on the tables here. They'll be gathered up and put on The Rescue and Gr – Mr. Peterson and Miss Murkle have promised to do their best to see that they are delivered. You may also send food packages, if you wish. They would have to be at the airport by 9:00 A.M. Sylvia and I are sending something by them to our boys. Goodnight, you guys and dolls. Don't forget I've called the Cabinet into special session at ten tomorrow morning. After that meeting I shall have a statement for the press."

It was eleven o'clock when the Wiremans and Grace and George were back in what Grace called the gubernatorial hideaway and gleefully predicted would not be a hideaway much longer "except as every home is the hideaway of the family it belongs to," because she was convinced that many Midwayans longed for something similar (perhaps already had it) or anyway would call it, when they knew about it, perfectly darling, simply adorable, and so nostalgic. Even George stayed up until midnight, saying he had slept most of the afternoon on a solid gold bed with solid satin sheets and solid purple velvet pillows and blankets.

"I dreamed I was an emperor," said George, "and all that bothered me, some way I felt as if I had to keep trying awful hard not to wish I'd turn into a fish like somebody in some old story. So it was kind of a load off my chest when Beaver come and woke me up."

Everybody laughed at that. It was very easy to laugh that night and they did a lot of it, even though the Governor was concentrating on practical plans he had to have formulated before the meeting with the Cabinet immediately after he saw Grace and George off in the morning and everyone kept interrupting with new ideas of what could be done and might and probably would happen just as soon as the people of Great Country were no longer confined to any one state but could move about freely again.

"All right, Granny," Beaver kept saying. "I know, Sylvia. I don't doubt it, Gramp. But you'll have to be patient. One step at a time. The first step is to make those Cabinet members think they have been coming to the conclusion for quite a while that what we ought to do for the good of the country, we ought to get the governors together."

"Maybe they have," said George. "Want to bet? A lot of 'em must know flowers used to smell pretty and wish they could find out whether they still do in other places."

"Well, I hope they have," Beaver said, "but even if they haven't it's up to me to try to make them think they have in time so that when I meet the press I can say the networks have been authorized to issue invitations to Governor Hurd of Two State, Governor Barton of Old State, and Secretary

Stiles of New State to meet with me at the Mansion this coming weekend if possible –"

George was irrepressible that night. "Will Bart have to sleep in that solid gold bed with the satin sheets and velvet blankets? If he will I won't let on to him about it, or he might not come."

"If he'll come, you can pick his bed, Gramp, and put a card in his breast pocket saying which one it is."

"I'll give Bart yours. I slept all right there last night. Felt like a bed. You're getting used to making do with a couch, I take it."

"If they'll come, I'll make do anywhere. Don't expect to sleep anyway. Probably won't sleep tonight either. But I think I'd better start trying, if I'm going to have a clear head in the morning."

"New State doesn't have a governor?"

"No. It's never had a government as far as I know. In the beginning they elected a spokesman, called here the

Secretary, but he neither speaks nor writes. At least we never hear from him, any more than we do from anyone else over there. Every few years somebody arriving in Two State reports to the Governor there that he is so-and-so who was the Secretary until he left and gives the name of the new one. Then that information is passed on to us. The last name I got was Stiles, Crossway Stiles. That probably came in two or three years ago. He may or may not be known by it there. I never knew the real names of the two before me who were Secretary there. Everybody called the first one Chief Leatherskin, and the next one King Cole. I assume those weren't their real names. I used to look for them after I got to Two State, but if I saw them did not recognize them."

"You've been head of every state you've lived in, Beaver?"

"It's nothing to be Secretary of New State. He doesn't do anything and nobody cares. It's a kind of joke."

"I suppose you told me you were,"

Sylvia said, "but I'd forgotten."

"It was nothing to remember, as I say."

"But, darling – did they call you by any other name than your own?"

"Sure."

"What?"

"I'm embarrassed to tell you. It didn't embarrass me then – nothing did – but it was probably supposed to."

"What was it?"

"Lord of Life and Love. If you must know."

"You were – and are – lord of my life and love," murmured Sylvia.

"Maybe it was prophetic," said Grace. "Tomorrow we'll go around asking, "Who's Secretary here now?' Won't we, George?"

"I'm counting on that. You are a just barely possible way of reaching him. I have no reason to suppose he or anyone else in New State turns on our broadcasts, so I'm going to ask you to take along several copies of a letter I'll send to him, explaining what I hope will be on the tube on every national hookup in twenty-four hours. Probably the best you can do will be to pass out the letters to anyone there who will take them. One might actually get to him. Now I'll go write it. And don't you think you'd better turn in, Gramp? It's midnight."

"Well, maybe I had better soften up that bed a mite more for Bart. He likes to take things as easy as he can, late years."

But Sylvia and Grace, in gowns, slippers, and filmy bedjackets (both Sylvia's, Grace had never owned one), sat talking on the sofa for another hour. Talked about what their world would be like if the Governors did agree to meet in Midway, and then maybe, together with their Cabinets, met in other states and eventually daily planes were scheduled to take any passengers who wanted to travel from any of the four states to any other.

"I should so love to visit you, dear Granny. We might find that my Uncle Bill and my aunts are still in your state. I think my brother Rob must be in Two State, if he lived. He hasn't reached here, I know, because I have carefully checked every list of new arrivals."

"And remember – if the time comes that we can visit, the planes will also carry mail, and there will be telephone connections at the borders – "

"Oh, yes. . . . Do you think people will want to use them, if they have them? Not just us, but many people?"

"Until many people want to use them, I suppose we won't have them. That's what Beaver means when he says to be patient. First he has to get the Governors to see that discussion of national problems is essential. Of course I know he will have no difficulty with Bart. But Governor Hurd may hold out a long time. Though he must be worried too. But he may not want Beaver to suspect he is."

"I think Beaver will want to meet with Governor Barton even if no one else will come."

"I hope so. I think he should. With

our new landing field that would be easy. Who knows, Sylvia? You and Beaver may be in Old State soon after George and I get home."

"Wouldn't that be lovely?"

"But that could wait a bit. It would be such a short first step. Much better if Governor Hurd will agree to come here."

"I don't really expect there is the slightest chance of your getting Beaver's invitation to the New State Secretary, do you? Much less of his coming? They all over there hate Midway more than anything. At least they did. Even I did – more than anything except New State itself."

"I know nothing about New State except what you have told me, Sylvia, I'm not at all imaginative and can't visualize a place or an atmosphere from what I've been told about it."

"I worry about you going there. And Gramp, too. Beaver could send messages by someone else. Now that he has decided to send messages."

"Maybe he will. But The Rescue is taking George and me to New State in the morning. It was in the agreement. It was part of the contract. Beaver promised Bart that we would go to every state. And I'm sure you have no reason to worry. Beaver assured us tonight that our two friends from Two State would be with us on the flight."

"You really trust them?"

"I had to, and from the first it was not difficult. Now I have as much confidence in Roddy and Max as I have in you and Beaver. I told Beaver tonight that, sorry as we shall be to leave you, we shall be very happy to be back with Max and Roddy."

"Well . . . since you will go, I'd rather you took our messages than anyone. You have some sort of rare gift, Granny, dear. If anyone can break down barriers, you can."

"I have little that anyone in Old State doesn't have. What younger people considered our crippling handicap is actually our unique asset. Age. I don't mean to imply that this makes us superior, overall, as the young have seemed to feel that youth made them. But it makes us different and so, for some purposes, invaluable. Just as, for other purposes, other groups or individuals are."

"I know. We need us all."

"Together. With our past and our present spread out like a book to be studied and constantly referred to as we chart the future."

"Yes. But I feel that if anyone can find – the Secretary, in the – the jungles of New State, it is you."

"It may be George."

"When I say you I mean you both. Now I must let you sleep."

"You sleep, too."

"I will. As soon as I pack some food. Goodnight, dear Granny."

"Goodnight. . . . And, Sylvia, surely you know the Secretary is not the only one I'll be looking for."

"I know. . . . You'll be looking for all those you have messages or packages for. And it may be – just may be – you will happen to find some of them."

"Or even one of them."

"Even one, Granny."

They were all up for breakfast together. Beaver and Sylvia went with their guests to the airport. It was a beautiful morning and they were all very gay. Max and Roddy were waiting at the foot of The Rescue steps. George shook hands with them and Grace kissed them. They were introduced to the Governor and his lady and they all shook hands. An official photographer took pictures.

"It's begun," Grace said to the Governor. "We've seen it start, and all of us will remember this morning. No more forgetting?"

"I could hardly refuse to promise you that."

Sylvia gave Grace two letters.

Max said, "This is a mail plane. They've stowed away eleven bags of letters. And more hampers full of packages. Sylvia said, "Mine are going

Special Delivery.''

She clung to Grace, stooping to do it.

''When you get home,'' Grace whispered, ''cry. When I get home, I'm going to!''

V The Kids

As the visitors from Old State turned at the top of the ramp from a final wave to Governor and Mrs. Wireman of Midway, they faced a tall young stranger in a gray uniform standing very straight and bowing stiffly.

He said, "Miss Murkle? Mr. Peterson? I am Ace Rafferty, your pilot. My instructions are to take you safely to whatever destination you choose. If you wish to go home at once, we can be at Old State airport in two hours. However, if you would like to return to Two State, I shall be happy to take you there, it is a flight of only a bit over an hour, and I have the honor of bringing you our Governor Hurd's cordial invitation to do so."

George had been waiting for a chance to shake hands with the boy and thrust out his hand just as the "boy" held out a square, official-looking envelope. Grace was suddenly reminded of the days when schools had graduates and principals shook hands with each as diplomas were being passed out. How often a graduate reached for that precious diploma with his right hand and was obliged to transfer it hastily in order to complete the little ceremony!

"Well, now, this is quite a surprise," said George, one eye on the envelope, "after being kind of rode out of there on a rail, you might say, night before last –"

"And we appreciate both Governor Hurd's invitation and your offer very much, Mr. Rafferty," Grace said quickly. "I hope that, as we used to say, you will give us rain checks on both. We should be delighted to visit Two State again very soon. But we must go home before then as we are on an assignment for our Governor Barton and must get our report in. And first of all we must complete the assignment by visiting New State. So that is where we wish you to take us today."

The pilot bowed again.

"That is a flight of close to an hour and a half. If at any time before I come in for a landing there you should decide to request a change of course, word will be brought to me in the cockpit."

He wheeled and vanished.

"Who'd he say he was?" George asked. "Captain Jinks of the Horse Marines?"

"The pilot. Let's get in and sit down so we can open that envelope and see if we can figure out what Governor Hurd is up to now."

But as they turned to enter the cabin they were astonished to find it nearly full of passengers, all young men, and all standing.

Max and Roddy grinned at them from the aisle.

"Surprise! Surprise!" said Roddy.

"Headquarters called for volunteers to go along on this flight," said Max. "Sixty-some volunteered but The Rescue has space for only thirty, including you. Some thought was given to using a larger plane – one of those in which we take the Kids to New State – but a larger plane could not positively assure a safe landing in Old State. Which is where we hope you will agree to go unless you will return with us to Two State."

"We are overwhelmed," said Grace. "If there are seats for us, may we sit down?"

"You are to take your choice of seats," said Roddy. "That's why everyone is standing. One reason. Just point the finger."

"What do you say, George?"

"Oh, somewhere in the middle. Where we can look both directions and see what we've got here."

"You would like to sit together?"

"No. I'll sit here with you. Why don't you sit across the aisle with Max, George? But pass me that letter as soon as you've read it."

"You might as well take it and read it. Likely you'll make more of it than

I would."

"Oh – I don't know which I want to do first – read or ask questions!"

"Read the letter first, Gram," said Max. "Then you can ask questions. And so can we. This is bound to be a talky flight."

Grace read. Then she asked if anyone on the plane knew the contents of the letter. No one did. The Rescue had started down the runway.

"Read it over the microphone, Roddy."

"You read it, Gram. They'd like to hear you read it."

"I can't. My throat would close right up if I tried. You read it."

Roddy went forward and read the letter aloud. As he read, Grace reached for George's hand but the aisle was too wide. He reached for hers and the two clasped in mid-air, not like those of teenage sweethearts, but thin, veined, brown, slightly misshapen, and quietly sustaining.

FROM THE OFFICE OF THE
GOVERNOR OF TWO STATE

My dear Miss Murkle:

It is the most sincere wish of the people of this state, as of myself and Mrs. Hurd, that you and Mr. Peterson pay us another visit at the earliest possible time. We hope that may be today, for several reasons. The first is that we greatly regret the misunderstanding which caused our recent breach of official hospitality and wish to make amends. There is a statewide sense of very real need for this to be done, as well as a strong desire for an exchange of views with you both, following your broadcast which passed our Board of Censors and went out in its entirety yesterday evening over both Two State channels. I judge you will be interested to know that young Charles Ryan and Dunwoodie Keogh are reported in excellent health and spirits this morning, and, along with other Two State children, are eagerly anticipating your next visit, which cannot be too soon for them or for us.

Our second reason for urging you to return today is that we learn from the crew of The Rescue that it is your intention to visit New State on your way home, and we urgently seek the opportunity to discuss this intention with you before it is carried out. We know much more about conditions in New State than the residents of any other state – even than its present residents, the conditions there being what they are – as none of us is more than twelve years away from it and a good many here now have quite recently arrived. We assure you it is most essential that you have the information, available here before you make the decision to touch down there.

Your safety, Miss Murkle and Mr. Peterson, has now become a matter of extreme importance to my people, and I must tell you that any threat to it, or any doubt of it, would set off activity on our part which would have serious countrywide repercussions.

We await word from your pilot that you will accept our urgent invitation and are changing course to be with us an hour or so from that time. Such a message will close all schools within an hour's bus ride of the airport, and you will be received by a large and enthusiastic delegation, including all the Keoghs and all the Ryans except Mrs. Ryan and the infant with whom she is only this morning returning from the hospital. The infant is a girl and is named Grace.

Assuring you of our keen personal interest in this matter,

Yours very truly,
Banner L. Hurd, Governor
The Sovereign State of Two State

The reading was followed by instantaneous applause from all sections of the cabin. The faces in front of George and Grace turned toward them, inquiring and friendly. The old hands separated, and the two leaned across the aisle to confer with each other. Then Grace went down to take the microphone.

"My throat is still tight," she said, "but I think I can keep it open. Your grandfather and I have never before had to refuse an invitation we wanted so much to accept. Let the word go to your Governor Hurd and all your people that, if it still stands, we shall accept it as soon as we possibly can. But as we see our obligation it is to visit New State and make our report to Old State before we revisit any state. In the meantime, whatever is known in Two State of New State must be known to you who have volunteered for this mission and are with us now. So we hope you will tell us, taking turns at this microphone, as much as you can about what you think we should know before reaching what we still feel should be our next destination."

Flight time passed quickly with the telling in persuasive, authoritative, insistent young male voices.

New State was a state of utter degeneracy in which there was security for no one; no learning, no industry, no ambition. There had been no repair or maintenance of any of the buildings, streets, roads, electrical, water, or sewer systems, or of any of the equipment and other provisions for civilized life regularly shipped in by Midway. The reason for this, of course, was that there was no discipline there of any kind, and the reason there was not and never had been was that from the day New State was incorporated it had been occupied exclusively by those who had learned in Midway to hate all discipline and the conformity, the misery, the emptiness created in the human spirit by discipline imposed upon it by forces for which it had no respect or liking or trust, only intense antagonism. Every influx of students had arrived in New State consumed by a more violent hatred of Midway than the one before, of everything it stood for and everything it had done to them. They came only wanting to do what they pleased, never again what anybody thought they ought to do, and to find out who and what they were. But every year it became more difficult to think of anything it pleased them to do, having run the gamut of self-indulgence and self-abuse; and of course nobody found out until he got to Two State who and what he was, because that is impossible without organized self-study, strict self-discipline, and standards and goals by which to measure one's progress. Not until he reached Two State did any citizen of Great Country suspect that he had a glorious primary duty to himself, to develop himself to the very limit of his potential, to earn the joyful knowledge of the feeling of self-pride, to instill these principles as much as possible into his children, and to acquire the power and skills by which whatever menaced his way of life could be beaten back and ultimately destroyed.

Nobody learned anything in New

State. It was wild, savage, mad, depraved, sick, hopeless, an absolute morass. Nobody but the very young and angry could possibly survive it, and many of them did not.

It was inconceivable that visitors from Old State could even communicate with them, not only because the language they used now was almost unintelligible even to those who had once lived there but also because they never had visitors, did not know what visitors were, and would react to visitors only in ways which, at best, would prevent anyone who went there from finding out any more about them than could be seen from the airport. If the visitors really wanted material for a report on New State conditions, the one way to get it was to return to Two State and interview its newest citizens, now held for gradual orientation in special institutions where interpreters would be provided and guards could guarantee personal safety.

"This is your pilot speaking. We have

crossed the Midway-New State boundary and shall be coming in for a landing in about fifteen minutes unless my instructions are changed."

Grace and George had held frequent conferences. Grace now went back to the microphone.

She said, "I think this has been what at least used to be called a careful briefing, and your grandfather and I are very grateful to you for it, as we are also for your volunteering to accompany us on what you are convinced is a dangerous undertaking. But we think it is both unnecessary and unwise for you and your state to become closely involved in this, our last stopover before returning home. It is Old State which conceived of this journey and made the arrangements for it. All the cooperation these arrangements required of our sister states was our transportation, our admission, and our safe-conduct. What you have been telling us is that you cannot guarantee our admission to and still less our safe-conduct through New

State territory. Old State does not expect you to. That is New State's responsibility, although as far as any of us know, its people are not yet aware of it. Midway cannot do it, any more than it could do it in Two State. I think Midway feared for us while in Two State as much as it and you fear for us in New State, though for quite a different reason. You both fear each other's organization as much as you fear New State's disorganization. We don't fear either. Perhaps there is good reason to fear New State. We don't know yet. But no reason is apparent to us why we should have feared either Two State or Midway. So we approach New State now only with intense curiosity, as we approached both of them in turn. Probably we are without fear because we accept the fact that we are expendable. The old fear little or nothing except death, which, fear it or not, they know is coming soon and may find them anywhere. What really matters is whether or not they can accomplish something more before it does find them. We are elated today because it is evident that we have already contributed something to the achievements of our state and therefore to those of Great Country. Enough so that word of it will reach home even if we do not. A foundation has been laid on which younger people can now build if they will. All that remains is to find out what, if anything, New Staters have to contribute toward a better world. Perhaps we are not going to be the ones who find this out. Perhaps it will be one of you later. Or someone from Midway. Or someone else from Old State. But now that we have come this far, now that we are this close, we want to try. All the other barriers have been broken, or at least cracked. Let us have our chance at breaking this one. We are not asking you to do more than plane crews usually do at the New State airport – land the plane and let off passengers, or land and pick up passengers. Only this time, if all goes well, it will be the same two passengers. . . . Can the pilot hear what I am saying?"

"Ace hears you, Gram," said Max grimly. "We're beginning to drop."

"Good. I have just one more thing to say. Please let us go in alone. And when we do, keep it in mind that you were all New State residents not long ago, and are finding that more recent arrivals from New State become good citizens of Two State. Isn't this proof that New Staters are not all bad, or hopelessly mad, or totally lost? That they are still people, as we found you to be and as you found us to be?"

"Come quick, Grace," said George. "Look out the window."

They were quite low now above the roofs of New State. Its stained, crumbling, obviously leaky roofs and walls; its broken windows, its streets riddled by potholes and littered with waste spilling over from alleys, back lots, sagging porches, and mountainous dumps; its open spaces crowded with figures lounging in the tall grass among low, sprawling, hungry-looking bushes, under dead and half-dead trees swaying in a wind.

"What s'pose them white patches might be up back of the city?" George asked.

"All I can think of is sheets spread on a hillside," said Grace. "Or tablecloths hung out. But that's because they're so far away. What are they, Roddy?"

"Outcroppings of limestone, I'd say."

"You've seen them before, of course."

"To tell the truth, I never look down much when we fly into New. Or back when we fly out."

"I mean when you lived here."

"No. Can't say I did. They're quite a way out. We kept pretty close to the cities. All Kids do."

"None of you ever saw those white patches when you lived there?"

"How about that, chips? Any of you remember seeing those white ledges, or whatever they are, before you left

New?"

All the young men looked out politely, shook their heads, and fixed their gaze again on George and Grace.

The plane touched down with a slight bounce.

"That's a new ridge," said Max. "We'd better have a look at it while we're here. Should have been reported. May have to get a repair crew sent over."

"Who runs this airport?" George asked. He was standing in the aisle now, hat on, rubbing his knee.

"Our company," Roddy answered. "It's such mean duty we all have to take turns at it. Each of us is sent over for a month about every two years. Nobody ever leaves the base. It's maintained like a fort, and Kids are never admitted except for boarding the planes to leave for Two. . . . Look, Gramp, Gram, it sure would be skrip if you'd give in just this once and let us ride you right out of here."

George grinned.

"They used to tell me you can't teach old dogs new tricks. I always aimed to finish what I started, and it's come to be a habit."

George patted Roddy's hand.

"You keep your fort, dear, and check your ridge, and do what you can to help out and cheer up the boys on duty here while we're gone. And don't worry. If we're not back in a couple of hours or so, we'll do our best to get a message to you. All we want to take with us are two hampers and two cases of letters."

The Rescue had rolled to a stop and the ramp was up. Its passengers emerged slowly, for George was very stiff. On the ground the Old Staters were surrounded by Two Staters.

"They still insist on going out alone," Roddy had told Max. "If they're not back soon they'll try to send a message."

"These are Miss Murkle and Mr. Peterson, chips," said Max. "They are going right out. Alone. May try to send in messages. Give them a buzzer code."

"Four long and five short, followed in about three seconds by two short."

"Sounds like what my father used to tell about twenty-party lines on the first country telephones," said George.

"I'm writing it down," said Grace. "Where is this buzzer?"

"At the gate."

"There's only one gate?"

"That's right. It hasn't been used for a long time except to let out Kids just in from Midway and to let in Kids going to Two State. The buzzer was put there for the use of Kids needing protection, and at first leaflets giving the code for that were dropped to them every few months, but it was never used except for mischief. I mean, if they buzzed that code number and the gate was opened, they only threw in rocks or garbage and went off when the hoses were turned on or the tear gas started. They were already bored with that in my time here. But four longs, five shorts, followed by two more shorts is your number, and, whoever buzzes it, the gate will open to.

Also there is a watchtower with telescopes and that will be manned as long as you're out. We'll keep our eye on you as much as we possibly can. If you're in trouble, and we know it, we'll get there as fast as we can."

"God forbid," said Grace, shaking her head.

"What does that mean?"

"Means I hope there never has to be a sudden confrontation between people who value discipline above all else and people who reject it completely. Even more I hope and pray that I may never be in any way a contributing factor in such an uneven struggle. So try not to come where we are if you can by any means see your way clear to wait a little longer.... Oh, look!" She quickly opened a hamper. "Yes, I thought so. Mrs. Wireman put in a red cloth. If you see us apparently in trouble, try to wait until one of us waves it as a signal cry for help."

"Food in there?" Roddy asked.

Grace nodded, smiling at him.

"You didn't cook it, though."

"No, dear. The Wiremans had a lunch put up for us –"

"Good," said Max. "Otherwise you would have had to eat here and it's Air Force chow."

"And Midwayans were sending in more all night, we heard. Special things their children used to like when they came on vacations. The packages have names on them. Just in case we should happen to find those particular Kids, as you call them. Otherwise we may give them to anyone who will take them. Of course we can't take with us all that were sent. Not nearly all. You don't know how lonely Midwayans are."

"They bring it on themselves," shrugged Max.

"No, not really. It began coming on Great Country even before the absolute division. That's what caused the division. But the division has added to it until it has become all but intolerable. You know that yourselves, but in Two State and in Midway you've refused to think about it. In Old State we have been left with little to do but think about it. What none of us knows yet is what the Kids of today are thinking about, or if they are thinking. And that's the next thing to find out."

All the passengers from The Rescue went with them as far as the gate which was a wall of impenetrable material resembling frosted glass. It lifted slowly. George and Grace passed through. The hampers were handed to George, the letter cases to Grace.

"Sure wish you wouldn't," Roddy said.

"Old folks can be awful stubborn," grinned George.

"Don't worry," Grace said again. "Everything is going to be all right."

"Be sure you're back here before dark at the latest," said Max. "There are practically no lights in New."

"You said two hours," Roddy reminded them.

"We'll try," Grace promised.

The gate dropped between Old

Staters and Two Staters, sudden and final as a guillotine.

"At last!" Grace said to George.

He set down the hampers, cupped his hands around his mouth, shouted, "Kids, we have come," and added a cracked yodel.

It was not a loud sound and when he made it the street ahead of them was as silent and deserted as if this were a ghost town. Only they seemed alive in what might have once been an undersea city from which its water cover had been sucked up by hot winds, leaving it to be gradually buried by desert sands which now the hot winds in their ceaseless, meaningless industry had blown away, leaving it cruelly exposed like the rusted, broken wheel of a long-lost prairie wagon and scattered parts of the skeleton of the horses which had pulled it.

But almost at once faces appeared in the old brick walls, staring down from windows without glass.

Grace waved and smiled. There was

no response.

"We want to see your Secretary," George called. "Where can we find your Secretary?"

There was no answer.

But now figures began filling empty doorframes at the ground level of the buildings. All wore breadths of cloth held together at the waist by large safety pins and covering them from there to the ground. The upper parts of their bodies were concealed only by their hair which apparently grew to whatever was its natural length, in some cases reaching only to the shoulders but most often hanging like a cape at least to the waist and sometimes to the area of the knees.

Grace opened her pocketbook, took out a letter bearing the gilded seal of the Governor of Midway, and said, "This is for your Secretary. For the head of New State government. We must find him and give it to him. Can you help us?"

The Kids only stared.

Grace picked her way briskly up a

broken walk.

When she was quite close to a group of ten or a dozen she pointed at them, smiling, and asked, "You are the Kids?"

Several of them slowly inclined their heads.

Grace pointed at herself and George.

"We are the Old. We came from Old State. The Old love Kids. . . . Do I use any words you use beside 'Kids'?"

After a minute one said hoarsely, "Love . . . Kids. Love . . . yes."

"Good!" exclaimed Grace cheerfully. "Let's see now." She held up Beaver's letter again. "Letter. Message. Message for the New State Secretary."

The faces remained blank, somber.

She dropped her cases on a crumbling step, opened one, and took out a handful of letters, spreading them like a fan.

"More letters. Messages. One for Alicia Ferreira. One for Oscar Somerset. One for Lida Hudlett. . . ."

She read a dozen or more names,

pausing and glancing around after each one, but saw no sign of recognition in any face.

"None of these Kids is here? You don't know anyone with any of these names?"

"Too stretch by double," said a girl, suddenly. She had thin, stringy, sandy hair which scarcely reached her shoulders and from her waist down she was swathed in green suede. "I'm Cat. He's Hands. She's Singer. He's Horn. He's Digs. He's Pip. She's Temp – "

Grace brightened.

"I see!" she cried. "You mean you don't call yourselves by such names as are on these letters. So even if you did know someone who was called Oscar Somerset when he lived in Midway, you wouldn't know him by that name. But you would know the name you were called by in Midway if you heard it, wouldn't you? When you lived in Midway, Cat, what did they call you there?"

For getting an answer to her question

this was the wrong approach – and perhaps there was no right one – but it did get a reaction. Cat smiled. Only a curl of the lip, expressing more disgust than amusement, but there was a trace of amusement in it. She spoke in a quick, low babble to those around her, some of whom then glared at Grace while others ducked their heads, covered their mouths, and made a sound like giggling. Then there they all were again, staring stonily.

"You might as well give up on messages, Grace," George called from where he was leaning against a tilted granite post. "Look here, Kids. In these hampers I've got better than messages to hand out to the right parties. Doughnuts, maybe. Drop cakes, I guess. Cookies, most likely. Stuff mothers baked that their Kids liked when they used to come home from school. They've got names on them, too."

He balanced a hamper on the post, turned back the cover, and pawed among the packages.

"Wool Friedland, Jr., I see here ... Dionid Lee ... Gloria Hathaway ..." He picked up a package and sniffed it. "Smells of chocolate. Brownies, prob'ly. Timothy Green ... Kera – Kera Masefield ... Hm. Spice. Cinnamon, I'd say. Dorian Wireman ... Seph – Sephus Crosby ... Finch Berry – "

A male Kid wrapped in carpeting material slouched out of the group, looked into George's hamper, and took a package.

"Just a minute now," George said. "They couldn't ever have called you Gloria, could they, son?"

"No show," the boy muttered. "She flits."

He took the package back up the walk and pushed it into the hands of a girl who had shaken her hair over her face. She ran into the building and he followed her. The rest stared.

"Tell you what, Kids," George said, opening the other hamper. "I can see you're honest. I'm going to spread out this cloth – "

"Keep it low, George," said Grace, apprehensively.

"Going to spread out this cloth and dump all the food packages onto it. You come look 'em over and see if any of 'em's for you or anybody you remember from school. Okay?"

They watched the heap grow. They all came and looked at the names on the packages. Nobody took any. Nobody spoke.

But they drew aside and mumbled together and then one, wrapped in a blue-striped sheet, said quite loudly, "Après moi," grabbed another Kid by the hand, and stared up the street. Her sheet was a twin to his.

Nobody else moved.

"Wht did he say?" asked George.

"Said to follow him."

"How d'you know?"

"It's French."

The two in blue stripes stopped at the end of the block, and the taller one made a come-on gesture.

Suddenly several Kids descended upon the packages, stacked them into the hampers, and picked up the hampers. Cat gave George a small push in the direction of the blue stripes. Nobody but George was paying any attention to Grace.

He said, "Looks like they mean we're supposed to go with them."

So she joined him, he took the letter cases, she rolled up the sandy cloth and tucked it under her arm, and they followed Blue Stripes.

"Glance back, George," said Grace.

"Jumpin' junipers!"

The group they had been trying to communicate with was also following, along with those who had filled the doorways behind them, and dozens, hundreds, who had been watching from windows in the walls. The Blue Stripes were so far ahead that George and Grace could barely keep them in sight, but thr following Kids were almost on their heels, so that from the Air Base watching it must appear that the Old Staters were leading a tremendous, spontaneous parade in which all the other participants wore costumes of floating hair and waist-to-toe shrouds cut from beach towels, bedlinen, and curtain, carpeting, upholstery, and suit and dress materials.

It was very hot and the walking was far from smooth or easy. George began to slow down, panting. Blue Stripes disappeared around a corner. Grace stopped, turned, and tried to spread her hands while still clutching purse and rolled cloth.

"Gone," she said. "We've lost them. We're old, Kids, and can't keep up this pace. Do you know where we are going? If you do, some of you will have to lead the way. And not so fast."

The Kids in front conferred. They laughed derisively. The word was passed back and the laughter grew. An instant later the Old Staters were the center of a galloping herd of half-human, half-animal creatures emitting half-human, half-animal outcries suggesting both children let out of school and cattle turned out to pasture, also the towering proud, blind rage of bulls and that lowest form of human meanness, the scorn of the weak by the strong.

Then the street was empty again, of all but the Old Staters and two girl Kids, one of whom had only one leg and walked on crutches while the other was racked by coughing.

The one on crutches said, "To Dice."

She paused to lean on one crutch and point with the other. George set down a letter case and shaded his eyes with his hand to look where she pointed.

"That – that old windmill?" he asked.

She stared at him, pointed once more, and started laboriously in its direction.

"Think you can make that, George?" Grace asked.

"I'll make it."

She reached for the letter case he had put down but he pushed her hand away.

"Better when I'm balanced," he said.

The girl who coughed had slumped to the curbing in a spasm. Grace bent over her.

"Have you anything to take for that, child? Any medicine?"

The girl shook her head, said "No dips – " and could get no further.

"Even some water might help. Do you know where there is water?"

She shook her head again, and said, "Boilo."

"I think you mean water has to be boiled for drinking. Of course it must. . . . Oh, dear, there is tea in one of the hampers. A bottle of hot for George and another of iced for me. But Blue Stripes have gone off with the hampers. . . . You poor child, here I am thinking aloud and you're coughing so you can't hear me and if you did you probably wouldn't make any sense out of it. . . . There must be some way I can help you."

But the girl could see that Grace was

staying with her while the other two inched toward the windmill on the horizon. She could feel Grace's hand on her back, rubbing gently, and hear the concern in Grace's voice.

Suddenly Grace remembered a few hard candies left in a package in her purse.

"Try this, dear. It's something. Just be careful you don't choke on it."

Sucking on the candy the girl was quieted, stood up, and really smiled at Grace, but it was a sad smile. She fixed her gaze on the hand she had felt at her back and touched it curiously with her finger.

She said, "Like – a mother."

"More like a grandmother."

"Grand-mother?"

"A grandmother is your mother's mother. Or your father's mother. You never knew your grandmothers but you had them. Two of them. They may still be living. In Old State, where I live, with all the other grandmothers and grandfathers. A grandfather is your father's father. Or your mother's father. . . . Are you really able to walk like this?"

They were rapidly catching up with George and the girl on crutches. There was no oral answer to Grace's question. She tried another.

"You said, 'Like a mother.' Do you remember your mother? Do you think of your mother sometimes?"

The girl coughed and said, "No dips."

"I don't know 'dips.' You used it before. About medicine. Does it mean 'use'? No dips – no use?"

"Don't know 'use.'"

"No – good?"

The girl looked faintly pleased, and nodded.

"No dips – no good?"

The girl nodded again. Their glances met in satisfaction. Grace felt as she might have if she had just mastered a basic stitch in knitting or crochet.

She said quickly, "I, Gram. You? . . . You?" The girl hesitated and then answered, "Mig. I, Mig."

They were now with George and the girl on crutches and had turned a corner. The old windmill stood just ahead as if on a teeming anthill.

"That is Dice?" Grace asked.

The girl on crutches turned and said, "He is Dice."

"Who is Dice?"

"Dice."

The Kids covering the low hill, filling every foot space, were swaying in unison. The effect was like that of a strange wind blowing tall grass a measure to the east and then a measure to the west, over and over, and there was the low, rhythmic humming such a wind would make. Then what was more like a giant birdcage than anything else the Old Staters had ever seen rose slowly from their center, inside the rusty framework of the old windmill, pulled on clanking chains until it lodged in the narrowing frame, high above the Kids' heads, perhaps twenty feet in the air. Inside the cage, on a tall-backed white chair upholstered in gold, sat a Kid who looked like all the others except that his shroud was of crimson velvet. As he rose, the rhythmic low humming from the Kids below increased to a mighty roar which died away to silence as he stopped and sat looking down on them.

When he spoke it was in words the Old Staters had never heard, or in phrases which were meaningless to them, but Grace recognized a wild, flowing poetry both in his rhythm and in the sound of his syllables.

He spoke, with frequent electric pauses, for perhaps five minutes, not so much to the other Kids as throwing a banner of unearthly color and texture across the sky above them. Until he stopped there was no other sound but his voice anywhere. An instant after he stopped the humming began again, grew to a roar, and died away again. For he had not descended. He sat there silent, still looking into the distance.

Then he said, "I've heard there are strangers here who use the language I am speaking now. Those who understand what I say now are to come to the foot of my tower. A way will be cleared for them and I shall meet them there. There are matters of which they and I shall speak.''

He added an unintelligible sentence, and the Kids directly in front of the Old Staters drew aside as if the wind blew in two directions from a gray spine stretching between the strangers and the windmill. At the same time the whole circle was drawing backward from the center leaving the base of the rusty old structure exposed. but only George and Grace noticed it. The eyes of all the Kids backing away were glued to its dangling occupant.

Feeling the first movement of the girl who coughed – though she had not while the Kid in the cage was speaking – and of the girl on crutches, Grace caught at the hand of the one and the shoulder of the other.

"Stay with us,''she said urgently. "Stay. Please. Stay. Wait. Be still – ''

But neither gave any sign that she heard. Their eyes were glazed, they mouthed the same chant as all the rest, and they moved as if pulled by an undertow.

Dice (a step backward); Dice (a step backward); Dice . . . Dice . . . Dice . . . Dice . . .

Grace, carrying her purse and the rolled red tablecloth, and George, having with a grunt picked up the letter cases, went forward alone to the base of the old windmill. As they went, the cage was dropping. As they drew near, the Kid swung out of it and opened a gate.

"Come on in," he said casually.

When they had, he closed the gate and lifted a trapdoor in the floor of the windmill and motioned them down a crude stairway.

"Why should we go down there?" George asked.

The Kid shrugged.

"Cooler, that's all," he said. "Where I live. If you want to sit down and talk."

"You live underground?" Grace

asked.

"Sure. Seen any better place? If you don't want to sit down, it's all the same to me."

"I do want to sit down," said Grace, "and I know we ought to get out of this heat. But Two State, under orders from Midway, is watching us through the airport telescopes and if they should see us suddenly disappear into the bowels of the earth, they might come rushing over here with six-guns blazing."

"Or their hoses and tear gas, huh?"

"Oh, the last thing we need is any mix-up like that," said George.

"Of course I did beg them not to come unless they saw me open up this red tablecloth and wave it for all I was worth – "

"But they're awful edgy, them fellers," George said. "Mean well, but edgy, so you can't tell what might set 'em off. Best not to take any chances."

"I know!" Grace exclaimed. "We've been gone almost two hours. We promised to try to send them a message if we weren't going to be back in two hours. Is there anybody you can send over to the airport with a message?"

"Sure. But whoever goes will get gassed or wet down."

"No, no. It's all planned out. They gave us a buzz code for the gate. They'll open to anybody who buzzes so many longs and so many shorts (I forget how many, but it's all written down in my purse) and take in any message we send, and be pleased to get it, too, I can tell you."

"Okay. I'll send it."

"All right, then. Now while I write the message, since they're watching us like hawks, could you do something to look like you're real friendly and having a good time together? You, George, and – what should we call you?"

"I'm Dice."

"Yes, that's what I gathered. And that's what we call you?"

"Call me whatever you like."

Grace nodded absentmindedly, fishing in her purse for a pen and note pad.

"Yes. . . . Oh, here's a place I can prop it. . . . Now go ahead like I said – "

George said something, slapping Dice on the back. Dice laughed and George laughed. George shook the rusty frame and looked up at the cage with the white and gold chair in it. Dice pulled it down a few more inches, which was as far as it would come, then up a foot or two. George grabbed the chains, tried to pull it down and couldn't. They both laughed again.

"Dear Max and Roddy and the rest," wrote Grace. "This is all most interesting. I suppose you saw the great crowd of Kids who brought us over to this old windmill. We are surprised and pleased to find that it is the home of a very nice young man who is – "

She looked up from her writing and asked, "Who can I tell them you are, Dice? Obviously you're somebody special. You aren't by any chance the head of the New State government?"

"There's no New State government."

"Then who are you? Or won't you say?"

"I'll say, but you can't tell them, or they'd be over here, for sure, bombs aweigh. I'm the New State god."

"Small g, I take it," said George.

"Either way. The Kids might use a capital. If they ever wrote it."

"But New State is supposed to have a Secretary."

"What New State has is Me."

"Then you must be the Secretary."

"Put it like this – if New State had a Secretary it would be Me."

"Good. You're Secretary." Grace wrote on. "New State's Secretary at present. He has greeted us cordially and invited us to lunch with him in his basement offices. They are located belowground at this season for protection from the heat. We don't know yet how long this conference will last, but in all likelihood we shall remain in New State at least two hours longer. With love from us both, Gram."

She folded the paper with a flourish, rote the buzz code on the outside, and as she passed it to Dice reached up and patted his cheek.

"Think nothing of that," she said. "I'm your grandmother and that's the kind of thing grandmothers do. Besides, it will further reassure the airport guards."

He pressed a button, and a Kid raced up out of nowhere on a battered, raucous motorcycle, received the paper and his instructions with lowered eyes, and raced away, flowered linen shroud billowing out behind him.

"Now once around this little compound, slowly," said Grace. "Of course, if you think you could bring yourself to put an arm across my shoulders, Dice – "

He said, "Easy," and they all laughed.

They felt the rusty supports of he windmill, shook them a little, talked, looking up at the cage.

"Now all right. I think we can go

down now. But *après toi*, Dice."

"Any idea what became of our hampers?" George called after him.

"They're down here," Dice answered from below.

"Why on earth were they brought here?"

"Because nobody knew what else to do with them. Or you."

Grace and George had reached the foot of the stairs. The room there had a smooth stone floor and walls, was wonderfully cook candlelit, and large. It had a long, heavy, carved oak table with eight matching chairs, and a couch in a corner. Water ran in a stream from an opening in one wall, filled a large crock, ran over into a stone basin, and gurgled into an iron pipe which carried it away. The hampers Midway mothers had packed were set on the floor, their packages, spread out on the table, names up.

"Sit down," said Dice. "I assume the thermos bottles and the unmarked packages are your lunch. Your friends abroad would hardly want you to eat our food. Actually, we have none except what they drop boxed. Very dull stuff."

"Then help yourself to some of ours, son," George said. "Chances are they packed a sight more than we can eat."

"I don't want what belongs to anybody else," said Dice, bringing three mugs of water from the overflowing crock and throwing himself into a chair. "Nobody here does. It's a New State – how do you say, virtue." He reached some distance down the table and spun a large package toward himself. "This is mine, if it's anybody's."

"It has your name on it?"

"What was my name, and never the name of anyone else who is here."

"Do you mind our knowing what it was?"

He had torn the paper from the white box and tossed off the cover. Looking down at the contents, curiously absorbed, he pushed the torn paper across the table.

He had torn through the name but Grace fitted the ragged edge together.

Dorian Wireman.

Dorian struck out in all directions. . . . Everyone who knew Dorian had reason to fear him, and did. . . . In despair they gave him up. . . . In his crimson school uniform . . . putting his sneering young face close to the plane window. . . . So the last I ever saw of my two children was Dorian's – Dorian's –

He was biting deep into a thick sandwich he had pulled from an insulating bag, looking with keen interest at the filling now exposed between the slices of dark bread, chewing noisily, washing it down with a long drink from his mug, and biting deep again, staring again at the filling with something like astonishment.

"You don't have to boil this water?" Grace asked.

It seemed a long time before he shot a bewildered look, first at George, then at Grace, and back to George again as if

incredulous that they were there, that he was not alone.

"Somebody say something?"

"About your water. A girl told me that New State water had to be boiled for drinking."

He grinned. "Not this. This is water for the god."

Grace and George drank from their mugs.

"Ice cold," said Grace. "Delicious."

"From an underground spring," said George. "No doubt about it." He turned to look at it, gurgling into the crock and splashing into the basin.

Nothing more was said until Dice had cleared his box of sandwiches and of what seemed to be at least a dozen spice bars with fruit and nuts in them and a very thin, transparent icing on top. George's and Grace's hunger had by then been satisfied for some time. They sat unnoticed, contentedly watching him.

When he did look at them again, embarrassment flashed across his face.

"Nothing a woman likes better than to see a man eat," Grace assured him. "Especially a young man. Especially if she cooked what he is eating."

"The Governor's Lady put together what I had," said Dice unexpectedly.

Grace nodded. "She sent you a letter, too. And I have one from the Governor to the Secretary of New State."

She reached for a case, found his letters, and slid them across the table to him. He did not so much as glance at them. He was tilted back on two legs of his chair, staring at the wall where the candles flickered.

"The Governor's Lady," he repeated slowly. "The Governor . . . the Big Boss. . . . They had the whole of Great Country in the palms of their hands. Still have it, whatever may be left of it. And never would even look at it, to see what could be done about it. Just clutched it. Still clutching it. Because all he wants is to be Boss, and all she wants is flowers to bury herself in."

"No, not all they want, Dice," said

Grace gently. "All they have. If anything, they are even lonelier than the rest of us. Their loneliness has become very close to unbearable."

Then he looked at her, quizzically.

"You think so? You know them, do you?"

"We have just spent two nights and a day in the Mansion."

He laughed at that, a cruel laugh. Both Grace and George sensed that his man's laugh covered a boy's sob.

"The Mansion!" He came down on the front leg of his chair, leaning forward on folded arms against the table. "Who are you, anyway? And why are you are here?"

They tried to tell him. He had heard no broadcasts either recently or ever since coming to New State; there was no power on which to operate any receivers which might still work. So they told him about the boys, the miracle of their reaching Old State, how Old Staters had seen this as an opportunity for a breakthrough and used it to get their first airport and at least one visit to each of their sister states.

They told him what they had seen and what had happened to them in Two State and in Midway. They could not tell it all. They told him what they thought was most likely to concern him, what he was most likely to understand.

Then Grace said, "Now will you answer some questions for us?"

"Shoot." That was what his father had said, Shoot.

"How is it that you speak the language we know? The other Kids say so little and what they do say is almost unintelligible to us."

"I told you I'm the god."

"Come now, Sensible answers," said Grace.

He laughed and said that when he came to New State his one goal was to get back to Midway someday and burn and smash until he had it on its knees to him, where he could mock it, and punish it, and maybe later make a decent place of it. He realized that if he was ever going to do that, Midway would have to understand what he said to it and he to understand what it said to him when he let it talk. So instead of trying to forget its language as the other Kids did – since it was hateful to them because of its associations – he had set himself to remember it and to learn more of it. He had not wanted to be with other Kids anyway. They had no more attraction for him than older people. He hated everybody. All he wanted was to get them all under his heel. So he had begun by hunting until he found this place. What a stroke of luck that was, coming on this dungeon with clean water under an old windmill! Next he ransacked the storage places – once called stores – until he found metal for fencing it in and bolts with which to lock it. For the first time in his life, being voluntarily imprisoned, he was free. Then he began bringing to it books from the libraries hardly anybody used any more, and read and wrote and read and wrote until he was nearly bursting from having no way to release it. That was when he got more metal and made the cage and fitted the chains with which he could pull himself skywards where he could let out his voice and not have it thrown back at him. By then those who had known him in Midway had forgotten him as completely as they had forgotten the language they had once used. They and older Kids heard his voice and came toward it. It was, he found, quite an effective voice.

"You have an extraordinary voice, Dice," said Grace. "Not especially in conversation, but when you let it out in the open air."

"So I don't often waste it on conversation."

Whenever he felt like it he had gone up there and sung out the great poems, scenes from the great plays, pages of the great literature of Great Country when it was a great country. And whenever he did, the Kids came swarming, though the words had no meaning for them, and all that got to them was the sound.

"And then what, Dice?"

Well, by then he had stopped wanting to burn and smash Midway. He had it figured out that it was destroying itself without his lifting a finger. For that matter, the whole country was down the drain and sinking into a bog. Whether other people knew it or not, he did, from reading what it had been doing and thinking hundreds of years ago. There was no need for him to bother about it where it was now. Besides, he had learned to like his way of life, locked into his shelter with pure water and the books ("I have two other rooms here. Both full of great books. Nobody else wants them. Nobody can read them") and with a cage he could ride toward the sky in, while still securely locked in; and whenever he did, a crowd gathering to say, "Ah – h – h – h." So he just got himself an armchair and painted it and upholstered it and rode up sitting down instead of standing as he had before. That was more comfortable. Also grander. The feel of the gold-colored velvet he used on the chair pleased him so much that he hunted for and found some in red to wear. It pleased him mightily to find that he wanted red, which once he had hated because it had been the color of his school uniforms. But they had been stiff, with high collars and scratchy gold braid. Velvet was soft. He liked red velvet and suddenly he wanted to be the only one to wear it. So he undertook next to figure out how he could reserve for himself all velvet that was in New State or would come into it in the cartons which at intervals rained down or were flown in from Midway and stacked outside the airport walls for anyone to take away who would.

"I guess I've got to interrupt," said George, fingering his watch. "Maybe this is as good a time as any. It's three o'clock, Grace. Hadn't you better send another message?"

Grace said, "Oh, what a nuisance!" and scribbled on another sheet from her notepad. "Can you get this over there for me, Dice?"

"Just have to run it upstairs."

"You'd better go up, too, Grace, hadn't you?"

"Yes, I suppose so. How silly it is! Just because nobody knows anybody who isn't just like them!"

She and Dice emerged together, he pushed a button, they stood talking, the motorcycle darted up and off again, they went back down the stairs, and George was snoring softly on the couch.

"I'm afraid he's getting very tired," Grace said. "but he won't give up. Old Stagers never give up, Dice. Let him sleep a while. Go on now. You wanted all the velvet –"

The way to get it seemed to be to make a claim to it, a claim that would be honored. He knew the Kid language, of course, and the Kid mores of which the main part was honesty. Having convinced himself that only he had a right to velvet he had now to convince them. This turned out to be surprisingly easy. He put into their language poetic myths he had learned of in his study of ancient peoples and ancient times. To do this he built new words to combine with those they had in such a way that the old words told the meaning of the new. It did require skill and time, but he had both.

Thus one day when he had gone up in the cage and sung out old poetry until a great crowd was assembled, he had amazed them all by speaking for the first time in their own tongue but with additions which struck their ears and drowsy minds as a clapper strikes a bell.

He told them that he was Dice, the Great Teacher, bringing them sweet knowledge of unknown forces which would one day lift them up as he was lifted up. Had he not brought them the joy of sounds such as they had never heard before? And he would continue to bring them more. Much more. He could not tell them what now. They would not understand if he did. As the days and years went by they would hear, they would see, they would feel, they would even taste beauty. But as he was to serve them, so they must serve him. It was one of the ways by which they would learn. From time to time he would have an assignment for them. He had the first one for them now.

Sitting high on the white and gold chair, he tossed in all directions small scraps of crimson and gold-colored velvet which they watched drift down and caught or scrambled for on the ground. This, he told them, was the Stuff of Dice and the scraps he now gave them were theirs to keep, to stroke with their fingers, to rub against their faces; a way of feeling what he felt and being near to him. But all large pieces of this Dice Stuff, in any color, whenever and wherever found, belonged to him and must be brought quietly at night to the foot of his tower. Some special good fortune would sooner or later befall anyone who found and brought it; and only they were ever to approach his tower except at the call of his voice.

It had worked out exactly as he thought. On pleasant nights he left the trapdoor open and if he heard movement in the grass outside and the thud of a roll or the rustle of a length of velvet he went upstairs and spoke in the dark with those who had brought it. He never took it in until after they had gone. By now his talking with them in that way was clearly reward enough. But from them he selected his Honor Guard, not only for their show of loyalty, their eagerness to be active under his command, and their superior health, but also for their skill in operating and servicing motorcycles. To these he gave the right of first choice among the new cycles delivered to New State annually, and no one questioned this right. He gave them also the right to draw daily from his water supply. In return they came when he touched the button and did as he directed. For over a year now no more velvet had been delivered to him, though his Guards told him Kids still searched for it. No new had been shipped in. Apparently he had it all. And it was nearly two years since he had been outside the windmill except to walk in the predawn hours when no one else was about. It was a life which suited him very well.

"And what are you going to do with it from here on? What is the next thing?"

Obviously the very next thing was to have the Guard find the Kids whose names were on these food packages. They could do it, wherever in the state these Kids might be. They were bright, tough boys, always ready for Dice work.

"This is a bigger job than you know. The hampers contained only samples. There are hundreds more at the airport. I'll arrange for them to be where your Guard can pick them up."

This brought out his delighted grin.

"Is that a fact! Then here comes that taste I promised them! I know that from my own experience. Even Kids who don't get it will hear about it. Very good. Very good indeed. It all adds up."

"To what, Dice?"

He shot Grace a quick glance and was sober, staring again at the wall.

After a minute she said softly, "And the letters? There are many bags of letters at the airport, too. Will your Gurd also see that they are delivered?"

He shrugged.

"If you like. The Guard likes to work. But only recent arrivals would be able to make any sense of them, and they would hate the sense they made. Few if any of them will be read. I'm vague as to why you want them delivered. Doesn't it occur to you that they may do a lot of harm? If anything, just make the Kids mad?"

Grace nodded slowly.

"You may be right. It's a great pity. It might be best to have the Guard bring the letters here. As to a post office. It is possible that someday at least some of them could be delivered. You could read them, if you would."

"I won't read them. They can be brought here, if you like, and stacked with the books. But I won't read them. They're not mine."

"Will you read yours?"

"I don't know. Not now. Maybe never. . . ." He brightened again. "But the food. That's taste. That's good."

"You said it all adds up. I asked you to what, and you didn't answer me."

His gaze went back to the wall, but, staring at it, he answered.

"Because I don't know. . . . It's what I think and study about all the time, of course. I've got everything I can think of that I want, that I could have, except that. A way to keep going this thing I've got. I can see that if it doesn't get bigger it's going to get smaller. If only I had more to work with, or could just think of something to work toward! . . . What I need is a new idea. A great new idea. . . . But it hasn't come. . . . Sometimes I think I'm not going to get it. . . ." Suddenly he turned angry, glaring at the wall. "Why do I have to, anyway? Why can't somebody else get a great idea? Why does everything have to depend on me? Let's face it. I'm just one of thousands of Kids! I read the books. I found pure water. I built the Cage. I gave them Sound. I got the velvet. I'm getting Taste to them. Why can't somebody else find something, do something, think of something, be something? Why does it all hang on Dice?"

Grace reached across the table and touched his big, boy's hand spread flat and hard against the oak.

She said softly, "It doesn't, Dice. It doesn't. And that very well may be your great new idea. Keep working on it."

George snorted, sat up, looked at his watch.

"Great balls of fire, Grace! More'n another hour gone. At this rate, it'll soon be night, and only two packages and two letters delivered."

"Who got the other package?" Dice asked curiously.

"A girl named Gloria Something. At least that was the name on the package she took."

"Gloria means nothing here. Stupid of me to ask."

"Dice is going to have all the

packages delivered, George. The letters, too, maybe, sometime. What better can we do with them than put them in the hands of the Secretary?"

"I s'pose that's well enough, but how we going to get them over here?"

"You said the Guard could pick them up at the airport," Dice reminded Grace.

"I'm sure they can. We'll arrange it as soon as we're back there."

"Send a message. It will get there faster and deliveries will start sooner."

"That's true." She began scribbling on another sheet. "Dear Roddy and Max, The New State Secretary is having his Guard call at the airport gate for the food parcels and letters we did not bring with us. They will come on motorcycles as the messengers have." She looked up. "How many motorcycles, Dice?"

"Better be fifty or sixty."

He came around the table and was reading over her shoulder.

"Probably fifty or sixty motorcycles," she wrote. "To speed

delivery all over New State as fast as the addresses can be located. Please advise Midway of the successful conclusion of these negotiations, as soon as the pickup is completed. Our conference with The Secretary will be ending shortly, and we shall return as soon as –"

"Wait a minute right there," said Dice. He was rubbing his chin. "Are they taking you to Old State tonight?"

"I hope not," said Grace. "There's going to be a lot of excitement when we get there, and in Old State excitement is more enjoyed in the morning."

"I'd like to get in one full night's sleep ahead of it, I know that," said George. "Nine o'clock's my regular bedtime."

"And I'd like to get my notes put together for the report," said Grace. "Haven't had a minute to do it yet, and nobody is going to want to wait for it to be written up after we get home. So I think we'll stay at the airport until morning. I gather there is not much more we could learn about New State if we should stay over tomorrow? Except for this it is all quite similar to what we saw on arrival? If so, I think we found out as much in an hour as we would in twenty-four. To see deeper and understand more, an outsider would need weeks. Oh – I had almost forgotten! I did want to ask what the white patches may be that we saw in the foothills as we were flying in. They looked from the plane like sheets spread on the grass to dry. The Two Staters supposed they were outcroppings of limestone, but had no recollection of them from when they lived here. They look quite far from any of the centres where they told us everyone congregates and stays. Have you ever noticed them? Do you know what I mean?"

"I can see them when I'm up in the cage," said Dice. "I've never been out there since it got started. But I know what it is. It's odd, your mentioning those 'white patches.' Because I was about to suggest taking you out there. It's the one thing that is different from anything else you've seen here. It's a –

well, it's what you might call a new development."

"You will take us out there?"

"If you get there, I'll have to take you."

" – we come back with the Secretary," wrote Grace, "from visiting a new development in the foothills. That is what those white patches are which we noticed as we were coming in to land. I assume you can follow us there with your telescopes and perhaps yourselves get an idea of what it is. In any case, there is not the slightest need of concern about us. The Secretary is showing us every courtesy, will afford us complete protection, and will have us safely back at the airport gate before nine o'clock. Please have Gramp's bed made up, and a table clear where I can write the report. With our love, Gram."

She folded the paper and Dice ran upstairs with it. There was the familiar churn and roar of a motor.

"He won't try to take us both on one

of them dang things, will he?" asked George.

Grace laughed.

"I guess that would wake you up!... No, if he doesn't offer more suitable transportation than that, of course we can't go. But let's see what he has in mind... You did get the idea, George, that he's the Wiremans' boy?"

"Thought must be, from what he said about his lunch. Quite a thing, wasn't it, our running across him this way?"

"Only that he's hard to miss, once anybody gets here."

"Same as no doubt his father was before him."

"Oh, he's a chip off the old block. I keep saying that basic humanity never changes – in a generation or a century or an age. All the difference there is is in what it has to adjust to – or thinks it has to adjust to."

"Trouble is in keeping on an even keel with all that putting on and taking off, dropping and picking up. Cargo ain't loaded right, boat'll founder."

Dice called down the stairs, "Your carriage awaits, my lady, sir."

"We leave these parcels and letters here?"

"I have one of each. They go where we're going. The others will soon be joined by those the Guard brings in. They'll check them by my files and get any steers they can before they start out."

Grace hurried up the stairs, George following more slowly.

From the top they saw the waiting "carriage" drawn up at the gate. It had apparently once been an open truck, but to its body had been added some of the framework of an ornate old house; below a sloping roof dripping white wooden lace there was a gilded door with stained-glass panels and on either side of this large but heavily curtained windows. A Kid at the wheel in the cab stared straight ahead. There was no one else in sight anywhere. These four might have been the only people in the world – the old man in the blue serge suit, white shirt, striped tie and soft hat; the old woman in a printed silk dress, little straw hat with a veil, beige nylons and low-heeled, laced brown shoes; the Kid of whom nothing could be seen but his dark hair and his profile; and the Kid with the very long fair hair and the crimson velvet shroud which swept the ground who was holding open the gilded door with the stained-glass panels.

Grace and George stepped in, Dice followed them, fastening the door with a bolt, and they rumbled off in a small room with a blue velvet carpet, bronze velvet walls, a gilded and frescoed ceiling, and several small chairs painted white, upholstered in gold-colored velvet, and chained to the sides of the room.

"Sit down quick, George," said Grace, "and hang on for dear life."

"Sorry Mick has to drive so fast," said Dice, "but it's quite a way and you want to be back at the airport by nine o'clock."

"I take it – this is – your idea of a

chariot."

The bouncing and lurching was nothing Dice minded. He talked as easily as he had in his dungeon, and more freely. He said nobody here wanted the cars sent over by Midway. They rusted where they lay. Most Kids now preferred to walk wherever they went. The rest used patched-up motorcycles. But some of his Guard thought there should be a conveyance in which he could ride without being seen if he should ever want to go anywhere in daylight. This was their idea of a proper chariot for the god. He had never ridden in it before, but he knew the Guard kept wishing he would. They had probably told the other Kids about it, told them to watch for it, that someday Dice might ride down their street or through the park; that though of course they would never see Dice anywhere but in the cage, if they ever saw that chariot moving they would know he was in it.

"Thousands of them are getting kicks right now," Dice said. "And they all need all they can get. I ought to have had it on the road before this."

But the farther they went the more restless he became. He changed from one chair to another, lounged on the floor, pulled at the tassels of the velvet curtains.

At last he said, "Well, we must be near enough so I should tell you what this is that we're coming to and how it got there. It almost certainly wasn't there when your Two State friends lived here. It's only been there two years. You might call it the first thing I did, when I was just starting to be Me. Even before I found the tower."

He went on to say that when he was haunting what was left of the libraries nearly everyone else had stopped using them, as they had stopped listening to the recording machines and all the other equipment set up here to educate them, since they had found so little to read which interested them and heard nothing they cared to know. But Dice (then known as Bull) was reading great literature, day and night, because he found it exciting; and there were two other Kids he often ran into in library corridors or heard through crumbling partitions. For a long time he never spoke to them. He had no more in common with them than with other Kids. Their being readers, too, was no shared interest because they studied only in the medical sections of the libraries. He knew this from overhearing some of what they talked about and read aloud about. After a while he began to get disgusted with seeing them around so much and hearing them talk so much, so he started to figure how he could get rid of them, have the libraries all to himself.

"It's when I think of something I want for myself that I get my best ideas," he boasted, rolling over on the velvet carpet.

So one night he walked in where the two of them – one was a girl – huddled over a book, holding a flashlight on it, and he told them point-blank that medicine and surgery weren't things to sit around and read and talk about all your life. After a while, if that was what you were interested in, you did something about it. He asked them how much they hated themselves, to sit here and talk about all this while Kids dragged around sick or fell down and died because the only place they knew of to go was the hospital, and everybody knew it was better to die outside than in. Nobody there knew anything about care of the sick. The Kids who "worked" in the hospitals were those who thought Love would cure everything. They didn't know one medication from another, and just let the filth accumulate; there was no surgery.

"'And here you two sit,' I told them," said Dice. "'Reading the years away. Do you care about this stuff you read or don't you? If you did you'd grab the books, get out far enough to find a clean spot, put up a clean shack to hold a few drugs and instruments, and at least stop a few earaches, just maybe even save a life before you close out and leave.' I gave it to them straight and I must have been good at talking even then, because the fact is that's what they did and I was so glad to get them out of the libraries I even helped them put up that first shack. After it was up I never went back, though. . . ."

He lay thinking for a minute, then pulled himself to his feet.

"Mick's braking. We must be almost there. When we stop, you two get out and start toward anything that looks like an entrance. Take it slow. I'll change into something one of my Guards would wear, and catch up with you. Dice is supposed to be waiting for us in here, you see. Nobody'll know me from a Guard. Call me Case, if you have to call me anything."

"We'll take it slow all right," Grace said in George's ear as she helped him up. "Question is if we can move at all."

Once on the ground they waited for their equilibrium and looked around in disbelief. The "white-patches" were a dozen or more one-story buildings, none really large but some larger than others, running up the side of a foothill of Great Mountain. All were of wood, crude but painted white, with whole, shining, screened windows, and between and for some distance before, around, and above them the land had been cleared and the grass mowed. The buildings stood as if on a soft green rug.

"Hear anything?" asked George.

"No. It's wonderfully quiet."

"My ears are the best part of me. I can hear a brook running."

As they approached a door, Dice joined them, in brown linen splashed with magenta flowers and blue grapes.

"Loely spot, Case," Grace said.

The door was open and a girl appeared in it. But what race of girl? Her hair was cut short, she wore a sleeveless white blouse, her white shroud ended well above her ankles, she had sandals on her bare feet, and her face shone.

"Hi, Kid," she said brightly, with an

inquiring glance at George and Grace. "Sick? Come on in."

"Nobody sick," growled Dice. "They dropped these. Two from Old State. Dice pitched."

"Oh, so you're one of Dice's Kids. Good. We can say more. Come on – "

Dice swung an arm toward the converted truck. Until then she had looked only at them. Now her eyes followed his motion and widened.

"Is He in it?"

"No go without Him."

"Oh, my goodness! Will He come in?"

Dice shook his head.

"No, I didn't think so."

"We want to see Doc."

"He should be down from the hospital soon. Come in and sit down."

"If we sit down now we may never get up," said Grace. "Could we just walk around until he comes back? We had quite a ride and old people get very stiff sitting. Gramp," pointing at George, "gets a cramp in his knee."

The girl nodded.

"I've read about that. Of course we've never had any cases. But maybe Doc and Annie will know of something we can do for it. Yes, go wherever you like. Do you want a – a –"

"Guided tour?" asked Grace, helpfully and hopefully.

The girl's smile flashed.

"That's what I was reaching for! I know what it means and how it looks in print but not how to pronounce it. Like a lot of nice words I either never heard or have forgotten."

"A guided tour is just what we'd like, dear," said Grace. "Then when we get back to Old State tomorrow we can tell all our friends about what you have here and what you're doing."

Dice held out a package and a letter.

"For Doc," he said.

"I'll leave them on his desk."

She stepped through an inner doorway and out again into the narrow hall which ran through the center of the building.

"This one is Admissions and Out Treatment. Never used as much as we'd like and nearly always empty at this time of day. . . ."

She went ahead of them, opening doors to either side, revealing immaculate little rooms bare of all but absolute essentials. By enclosed ramps they climbed to the maternity ward where white baskets were set in racks beside the white beds of three mothers, of whom one looked frightened by the visitors at the door. The other two were sleeping.

"Old State dropped," the guide told the frightened one, gently. "Pick up soon." She looked at her watch, tapped it, and smiled. "Lou. Soup tonight. Salad. Ice cream."

The kitchen, all white, where Kids dressed like the guide were setting up trays and kettles steamed over wood fires. . . .

"We get our wood from the mountain," said the guide. "There's no end to it. The mountain is always growing more."

The operating room, which made George think of stories he had heard about surgery performed on kitchen tables . . . the surgical ward with two patients, one with face to the wall and the other sitting up in bed, looking at the pictures in a magazine.

"And now the Fun Places," said the guide.

They followed her outside and across the grass to one after another building with rooms full of babies being given their bottles, either held by Kids dressed like the guide or lying dreamy-eyed in small beds with the bottles propped against pillows. ("They get turns being held.") Other rooms had long tables around which older children crowded, eating with spoons from bowls and drinking from mugs while a Kid in white played a guitar and sang.

"So this is what's become of them," said Dice.

"You've missed them down there?" asked the guide brightly. "Well, you see, if a Kid comes up here to have one, she's likely not to want to take it back with her when she goes. Or if she brings up a sick one and it gets well, she wants it to stay. Quite often she stays, too. That's how we've built up our staff. Nibs?"

He nodded.

"Okay. Now we didn't catch sight of Doc and Annie anywhere. Let's see if they're back in the office. . . . Yes, here they are. Doc, you may find this hard to believe, but a couple from Old State have been dropped here and they wanted to see our spread. They came up in Dice's Car, and – "

"Annie saw it out there," said the man in white behind the desk. "We've been out trying to find out if he's in it but the Kid at the wheel won't speak and threatened us with his fist when we started toward the door. Who left that package and the letter?"

"The Kid who came in with the Old Staters, Doc."

"What I want to know is how Dice

came by them."

"How about that, Kid? Do you know? . . . If he does, he won't tell, Doc. All of a sudden he won't speak, either. Though he's been speaking – "

"I can explain the package and the letter, Doctor," said Grace. "They were among a great many sent by us when we flew in from Midway this morning. We have been on a visit there, and Midway people, knowing we were going to stop over in New State on our way home – "

"You are Miss Murkle and Mr. Peterson, mentioned in the letter. A most extraordinary thing you have done. I wish I had time to go into it with you, but matters of extreme importance with which I am deeply concerned must be dealt with immediately. You have given me a rare opportunity to do so. I have long tried by every means I knew to contact Dice or any of his Guard, but without success. Lock the door, Annie. Kid, that door cannot now be opened except by one who knows the combination. Now you listen carefully to this message and repeat it as accurately as you can to Dice. I assure you he will listen."

The message was that only the Doctor and Dice knew who the Kid was who had envisioned the beginning of this hospital and helped to raise the first building. He had since disappeared, but they knew who he was and why he had done it. Also why he had disappeared. And knowing that, how could Dice, with all the influence he had, go on letting so many other Kids and their babies die down there, or live too sick to care? Bull's Kid was only the first one that didn't get up here in time. That was bad enough. Why was it going on and on and on? Why didn't Dice put a stop to it? He could get up here everybody who was sick, if he tried. All he had to do was tell them to come. But first he should come himself, see what was here, and start by sending up as many of the sick as the staff could handle. Maybe then he would send the Kids and material to build a training school, and Kids to be trained in it, and other Kids to put up more buildings where the new trainees could take care of more of the sick. New could cover the whole side of Great Mountain with schools and hospitals and sanitariums and nurseries and libraries until everybody had been pulled out of those filthy cities. Then, when they knew how, they could begin cleaning up the cities. Kids could build a whole fresh new healthy world. But they had to begin with themselves. Dice could make them see that, if he would. So why was he satisfied to just hide down there in his dungeon and ride up out of it once in a while, say something pretty, and give the Kids a few new words they didn't know what to do with after they got them? What kind of a god was he? Why didn't he read a little more about what gods used to be and do? Had he ever heard yet, for instance, of the God of the Hebrews?

He paused at last, and Grace said quietly, "If that is all of your message to

Dice, Doctor, I think we should go now. I have a report to write tonight and we shall take off for Old State quite early in the morning."

He turned toward her. The strain of the effort to change his line of thought showed on his face.

"Annie and I very much regret that you cannot stay longer. I trust you understand why we could not be more hospitable at this time. The hour is almost unbearably exciting. I feel currents I have never felt before. I cannot tell yet which of them come from you and which from what you brought to me from Midway. I have not yet opened the package but can guess what it contains. Annie has read the letter and we wish to reply to it. Is there a way by which we can get a letter on your plane, to be delivered when it returns to Midway?"

"At least until we leave, the airport gate will open to the buzzer signal of four longs, five shorts, followed in about three seconds by two more shorts. Shall

I write it out?"

"Annie has written it as you gave it. Thank you. I hope you will come to us again, Miss Murkle . . . Mr. Peterson . . . I feel you will."

Annie, dressed like the guide, rose from the desk and went to the door with the visitors. There she tipped back her close-cropped, golden head to look Dice in the eye.

She asked, "You will come back? You will think about talking with him?"

"I'll be back as soon as I've started these people toward the airport. Go in and tell him so."

"Oh – bless you, Bull!" Suddenly she kissed both Grace and George. "Bless you, too, for getting him here – and for all Doc feels that we can't even name yet."

As the three went toward the chariot in the dark, Grace found Dice's hand and said, "It wasn't quite the way you told us, was it, that this hospital got started?"

"It was the way I wished it had."

"At the time. Because the girl you loved didn't live to use what you had started for her. That made you bitter. And Doc and Annie were up here together and you remembered their voices in the library, especially her voice reading aloud. You thought you hated them. But there was nothing to hate them for, was there? They are working out that dream of yours in the only way there is. You told us you need people who have ideas, and now you have some. You and Doc are made of the stuff ideas come from. Together you will find others. We shall be waiting to hear what happens next. So much is bound to happen."

"Take the Old Staters to the airport gate, Mick," said Dice. "Then come right back here and wait."

He followed them up the steps, shook hands with George, and hugged Grace roughly. She clung to him for a minute.

"I want to ask a favor of you. There's a girl they call Mig on that street we came in on this morning. Get her up here as soon as you can. She has a terrible cough. . . . We all know you're no god, Dorian. But you're a fine, dear boy. Do think about going to the Governors' meeting."

The door with the stained-glass panels closed. The chariot lurched forward.

"Well, here we go again," said George. "Headed for the last lap. . . . Been quite a thing, but I won't be sorry when it's over. I'm most beat out."

"I told them to have your bed made up. You'll be chipper in the morning."

After a while George said, "What I can't figure out is why if he was going back and talk to the doctor he wouldn't say a word while he was there."

"Because he was pretending he was Case instead of Dice, and the doctor knew Dice when he was called Bull and might recognize his voice."

"Hm . . . If the Doc would know his voice, wouldn't he know who he was, by looking at him?"

"No. Because the doctor is blind."

"Blind! I didn't notice that."

"I didn't think you did. He's very skillful."

Some time later George said, "But that Annie. She knew he was Dice and Bull and all the rest of it. Why didn't she tell the Doc?"

"She didn't think it was her place to. Dice counted on her sensing that. It had to be between Dice and Doc. They're brothers, George. They're the Wireman boys."

VI The State and the Nation

"As we saw Great Country it was still sharply divided into four states. We were the first travelers to cross the land boundaries of all four in forty years, or since those boundaries became not only legal but physical barriers between the four age groups who found themselves forty years ago so cut off from one another emotionally and intellectually that they decided communication had become impossible, except with contemporaries, and that complete separation was the answer for all, save only young children and their parents. It has long been assumed, erroneously, that this was the unanimous decision of the people. Actually it was the decision only of the majority, but the majority of all voting age groups – young parents who did not want their children spoiled by grandparents, the middle-aged who did not want their young people confused and retarded by outdated ideas, young people who had lost confidence in and respect for all ideas except those they originated (or thought they had), and old people who were tired of trying and wanted only peace.

"The decision was made and implemented. We have seen the result of the Great Experiment, based on the desperation which led to it.

"A vast and terrible loneliness has gripped this land. It is shaken by fear as by earthquakes. Its store of knowledge has terrifyingly diminished. It has buried the old ideas and there has not been a new one for decades in all its circumference.

"In New State children are born in squalor and, if they live, live in squalor until they go with their mothers to Two State and there may or may not gain fathers. In any case, all new arrivals in Two State are subjected to what amounts to imprisonment for a process known as orientation, which is in fact one of indoctrination to a way of life more civilized than the children have ever known or than their elders have known since leaving there at the age of twelve, but also far more regimented, more comformist, and so more barren; those between the ages of thirty and forty are on the whole more dictatorial, more driven to impose their customs on others than older or younger people.

"At about the age of twelve the child leaves New State for school in Midway. His parents may or may not go with him. It matters little to him. He goes into a new prison, subject completely to the influence of his teachers and his fellow-pupils, of which his parents know nothing and over which they exert no control. They must now begin to live without him. What is there for such people to live for, for twenty-five years, except power and luxury (of which one quickly tires), the relief of forgetting (which becomes increasingly difficult to obtain, leading to greater and greater excesses), and the false hope of joy in retirement?

"Meantime the preparatory school student – now for four or five years to all intents and purposes an orphan – arrives in what was once the college and graduate school community. It has not had anyone over the age of thirty in it for forty years until today, and even today only two sightseers from Old State. There has been no repair of its buildings or its equipment, no organized study, no progress, only steady deterioration and recourse to the primitive. Even the knowledge of Great Country language has all but disappeared there, blocked out by choice and because memory, like other responses, has been curiously impaired by the habits of the residents, their way of life. Small wonder that those leaving here after a dozen years of such an existence are regarded as savages.

"All round and round this has been going, like what some Old Staters will remember as the wheel of a vehicle spinning in mud. It is what most Old

Staters in their isolation have suspected, but hoped was not true. It is true.

"However, having thus led you along the streets of our nation, we can now show you that, even after all these darkening years, the light has not gone out. It is still visible in every section of our Great Country.

"Light came into Old State with the miraculous arrival of two small boys who had just seen it above the treeline of Great Mountain, where they were the first human beings to go in more than a century.

"We saw it in Two State in the devotion of the parents there to their small children, in the degree of civilization they have attained, in the fact that something of one of Elder Walmsley's churches remains and is still cherished though not understood, and in the growing friendliness shown to us by its people who were encountering the old, and the views of the old, not only for the first time but under for them alarming conditions.

"We found it in Midway in the very loneliness of parents for their grown children and for the grandchildren they may never see or even know they have; and in the love of at least one husband and wife for each other, in their constant search for a way out of what has seemed a hopeless tangle of the affairs of men. Could we have stayed longer and come to know more Midwayans personally, we should no doubt have met others like them.

"It shone most brightly in what all assumed was the darkest spot. In New State where its people now speak almost entirely in words of one syllable there is one who is giving them the sound of great literature, poetry, and drama and gradually reviving the national language there; he is also awakening them to a vague sense of their spiritual need, whether he knows it yet or not. There are also two who have climbed as far as the foothills of Great Mountain and built a little white 'city on a hill'; a clean, gentle, and kind little city; a place of primitive healing. And even in one day we saw that many are groping for what these three offer and for the source of it. They are young, with much left of the very special qualities of youth. One of them told us today, 'The hour is almost unbearably exciting. I feel currents I have never felt before.' We felt them, too.

"Only time and events yet to come will show which state has the most to offer to a reunited country. If we were obliged to name tonight the one closest to an extraordinary breakthrough, we should have to say New State. But, without much to draw on that other states have, even New State dreamers will succumb to disillusion, as without access to the purity of its dreams the rest of us are already doing.

"The barriers must come down with all haste. The experiment has been tried and proven a tragic failure. Great Country is no longer a great country. It is almost a lost country. But we are not completely lost while we still see light.

"As we in Old State believe, as two small boys in Two State know, as the Governor's Lady in Midway feels, and as many in New State are beginning to sense, the Source of all light is somewhere above the treeline of our Great Mountain and will never fail us.

"Let us now be quickly about our task of not failing the one true God, the one Great Teacher, the one Great Physician, the one Great Governor, the one Great Unifier of all ages, all races, all varieties of those He created, in His infinite wisdom, in His image. When we turn away from Him we turn away from one another, and as we turn from one another we turn farther away from Him. This is the truly intolerable loneliness. And it leaves Him lonely, too.

"Grace C. Murkle
"George T. Peterson"